I0587457

Moments of Darkness

Tales of hauntings, nightmares, murder and
imagination of the darkest kind.

by

Christine Lawrence

Cover design by Jan Stephens

The Froddington Arms

It was a dark night and windy. I had walked across the marshes from Portsmouth town, keen to get away from the fevers, the evil humours from the effluence left by the King's army. I'd spent half the year in Portsmouth, working day and night plying my wares to the troops, hoping to make enough sovereigns to take home to our farm in the northern end of Portsea Island. The farm was failing, the crops had been confiscated by the soldiers as they passed through to Portsmouth, our grain stores purloined to feed the sailors of King Harry's fleet, the fleet still waiting to sail against the French who were readying to attack our shores. I had to earn some money somehow so had gone into Portsmouth and sought to make enough money to feed us for the winter, hoping to buy enough grain to plant for the next season. The streets of the walled town had been heaving, crammed full of troops, sailors, merchants and people like me, selling their bodies for pennies in any alleyway all over the town. Alas, not much had been earned as the soldiers had yet to be paid.

It had been early Spring when I'd arrived in the town and the cool sea breezes blew away the evil mists but as the year progressed, the wind had dropped, more and more troops crowded in and no provision was made to clear the cesspits on the edge of the town. Diseases began to spread and by September I decided it was time to leave. I was reluctant on one level as there were promises of the troops being rewarded by the King with still money to be made. The troops were bored and waiting for action. I hadn't made nearly enough to see us through the winter but couldn't risk the fevers, so here I was, footsore and weary, late evening in

Froddington, entering the only inn I could find in this poor hamlet, hoping for a bed for the night.

The room was dark, lit only by the open fire; a kettle hung from the chimney on a chain, steam hissing from its spout. I'd been inside for a few moments before I noticed the three men who sat in a corner on the far side of the room. Beyond them, leaning across the bar, was a large woman, her huge grimy bosom forming a shelf resting on the counter, her lank hair escaping from a greasy mob-cap. She smiled a toothless grin across at me as I approached the bar.

"Well child, you've come at last. You'll be looking for a bed for the night, then?" She winked at the shadows. "You can call me Meg." It was only then that I noticed the man in the darkness at the end of the bar. A face loomed towards me - I felt the stink of his breath before I met his eyes and in that moment I swear I saw a glint of red flash from them. I wanted more than anything at that moment to turn away and leave but something seemed to hold me there, in some kind of spell. How long I was held there, I cannot recall, I seemed to be falling into the deep pools of his black eyes. The magic was broken by the sound of a tankard slamming onto the bar and the deep laughter of Meg.

"Here, you'll be needing refreshment no doubt," and in that moment as I turned to her I felt a cold chill rush across the back of my neck.

"Thank you, yes, and a little bite to eat, if you please," I replied. The woman ambled away through an arched doorway at the rear of the room. Unwilling to be left alone with the dark-eyed stranger, I moved to the warmth of the open-fire. When I'd settled onto a wooden stool near the hearth I glanced back to the bar but the man had gone. This was the first time I thought, how strange - no way out unless he'd walked past me or leapt over the bar.

I was still troubling myself with these thoughts when Meg returned with a bowl of broth and a hunk of dry bread. My hunger got the better of my curiosity and I was soon devouring the meagre meal with relish. After washing it down with the tankard of ale, the weariness of the day overcame any concerns other than where my bed would be. As I rose to follow Meg up the narrow stairs to the bedchamber, the three men were still in the corner, arguing over their dice-game. They didn't seem to notice that I was even there, and still no sign of the man at the bar.

Meg pushed open a door and we entered the room, sparsely furnished with a large four poster bed on one side of the room and a chest pushed against the opposite wall. On the chest was a bowl and jug of water for washing; a linen cloth hung from a hook on the beam above the chest. The only window was un-curtained but tightly closed and the new moon could just be seen hanging in the dark sky outside. The flickering shadows of a tree danced in the weak moonlight on the walls of the room.

"Here you are my dear." Meg handed me the candle that had lit us up the stairs. "We haven't had many guests recently but you'll find the bed well-aired." She chuckled to herself as she turned her back on me and stomped back through the door and down to the floor below. I was far too tired to wonder why there had been few guests in this busy time on this small island and soon sank into the softness of the feather-down mattress.

Sleep came easily, fueled no doubt by the strong ale I'd consumed so I was alarmed to be woken so abruptly only a short time later. Or at least, I assumed only a short time had passed. The moon remained in sight from my bed and the shadows of the tree flickered on the walls. Still wondering what had woken me from my slumbers and a little frightened to look about the room, to tell the truth, I felt that chill across my face, the same chill I'd felt in the bar earlier. I wanted more than anything at that moment to hide under the covers and pretend that there was nothing there. Something however compelled me to turn my head and look about the room. Fear leapt at me as I saw the dark-eyed stranger standing at the foot of the bed, his eyes flashing red again. I hadn't imagined it before and I wasn't imagining it now.

"Don't be afeared," he whispered. "I knew you'd come in time. I've waited for so long."

"What do you want?" My voice was shaking. Was this just another man after my body, or something else? To tell the truth I was sick of degrading myself for money although the thought of earning a few more coins was always welcome and I'd grit my teeth to get us through the winter.

"Don't worry, it's not your body I'm after - not in the way you think, anyway." He smiled, a haunting shadow of a smile. "I need your help, that's all. Come with me and you'll be well rewarded."

Well, the last thing I wanted at that moment was to leave the warmth and comparative safety of my bed to follow this awful-looking stranger. I tried to resist but something made me rise from the bed and still dressed I slipped on my shoes and followed him from the room. I had a passing thought that the floor-boards creaking under my feet were silent as he stepped over them. Soon we were in the lane outside the inn. Without even pausing to check that I was following, he moved on past the darkened cottages and down the lane towards the old church yard.

Ghostly fingers lingered across my face as we passed under the lych-gate into the shadow of the church. I stifled a scream. It was only a trail of ivy, loosened by the wind. I scurried on, trying to keep up with my guide, wanting more than ever to just be gone, back home to our farm but I couldn't stop myself and followed him until we reached the darkest corner of the cemetery, under an ancient yew tree. Now, yew trees have always brought me into a state of calm and I could feel myself relax a little. I remembered their purpose, to keep away evil spirits so why was I being brought here? Almost as soon as I had that questioning thought in my mind, the answer was there.

"Look under the turf at the base of the headstone; there you'll find what I am seeking."

It was more of a thought in my head although at the time I was sure he'd spoken. I knelt by the grave and dug with my fingers into the soft earth around the base of the stone. The grass was growing thicker here but I somehow managed to make a hole with my bare hands.

"Dig deeper," I heard in my ear and as I turned to him impatiently his eyes seared into mine. "It's there, you'll need to dig deeper."

"What exactly are you looking for?" I muttered to myself as I turned back to the task. "And why me? Surely you could have done this yourself, any time."

"Just dig, and all will be shown to you. Dig, and when you've found it I'll tell you what to do next."

"It would be easier if I had a light and some tools," I complained. As I spoke the evergreen branches above us seemed to part, shining thin moonlight onto a flat stone lying there on the grass next to the grave. Poor light indeed, but just enough to see clearer what I was doing. Soon with the help of the flat stone I was able to dig easier and was shovelling the soil from the hole.

"Be careful. It should be just there. Use your hands only now." The stone fell from my grip and I felt around in the dirt. There was something there, hard and smooth and about the size of a coin. I felt all around the edge, carefully scraping away the soil.

9

As soon as I'd uncovered it completely I managed to lift it from its earthly grave, shaking the loose soil from the long chain attached to it. It was a locket.

"This what you want?" I held the shiny artifact up to show him, thinking he would snatch it from my hands but he just sat on a nearby gravestone and smiled.

'Thank you. Now for the next part of the task,' he said.

"Now, wait just a moment," I protested. "First you must tell me what this means. Is this yours, and if so what's it doing buried here? And why couldn't you just have got it yourself?"

I held up the locket watching as it spun, gradually slowing almost to a stop. Then without any help from me, it began to swing to and fro like a pendulum as it if had a life of its own. I looked from the locket back to the stranger. His eyes were even deeper, if that were possible.

"Well? You haven't answered my questions. You knew this was here. You could have collected it at any time without my help." I thrust the trinket at him thinking he would snatch at it but he stepped backwards away from me as though afeared of my touch.

"No!" he snapped. "I can't touch it. You must carry it for me." He stopped. I waited.

"I'm not moving until you explain." I felt suddenly brave and wondered how he'd persuaded me out of my warm bed to this dark graveyard. My determination only lasted a moment however, as he stood over me then turned to move away - I felt an overwhelming urge to follow, still clutching the chain and locket in my hand.

"Where are you going?" I called but there was no answer. He led me out through the lych-gate and into the lane, turning back the way we'd come. I walked as though in a dream along the narrow leafy bridleway until we came to a halt in front of a pair of high wooden gates, tightly closed to the outside world. I wondered how we would get inside, if that was indeed what he intended. The gates were chained together and padlocked. The lock and chain were rusty and looked as though they'd not been opened for years. Then I realised that there was a gap at the side of the gates where the wall had crumbled. Without speaking the stranger made his way to the gap and whilst I was still wondering what I was doing there, he appeared to glide through to the other side. I felt myself compelled to follow and scrambled over the fallen stones.

Once inside the atmosphere seemed to have changed. The air was still, the trees no longer buffeted by the wind, all was quiet. Then I saw the house. A gloomy affair with thatched roof and small windows. I thought that it was uninhabited until I noticed a candle in one of the windows under the eaves. My stranger had stopped and was staring at the light. Then he turned to me.

"Knock on the door and give the locket to the person who answers," he said. I hesitated, unwilling to waken the poor person living here. "Knock," he persisted. "Then all will be revealed to you."

I stood in front of the door and knocked. "Louder," he insisted. "Louder." I knocked again, louder this time and stepped back to look up at the candle light in the window above. A woman's face appeared in the light so I waved. The woman disappeared along with the light. I could hear the sound of footsteps on the stairs inside and finally the door creaked open. An old woman stood there, her long white neatly plaited hair reached below her waist.

"What is it?" she looked puzzled. "I haven't had a visitor here for over forty years. How did you find your way in?" She paused, waiting for an answer. When none came she went on, "Well, you'd better come in and explain yourself."

She opened the door wider to let us in. Before I went inside I turned to look at the stranger but he'd gone. I seemed to be alone with the old woman. "Wait," I said. "There's a gentleman with me. He led me here."

The woman stepped outside and looked about. "Well there's nobody there now," she said. "He must have gone away." She came inside and ushered me to the fire-side. "Sit here and tell me all about it," she said.

"He wanted me to give you this." The locket was still entwined around my fingers. I held it out to her in the dim light of the glowing embers. She gasped as she reached for it.

"My locket." There were tears in her eyes as she held the locket to her lips. "Where did you find it?"

"It was in the graveyard, buried at the base of a headstone."

"What headstone? What was written on it?"

"Sorry, I don't know. Look, I don't know what all this is about. I just got taken to the church yard by this man and told to dig until I found that locket. I'm staying at the Froddington Arms, just for one night, on my way home. I didn't want to do any of this but..." I paused, wondering how to explain how I'd got involved in this mystery. "Look, it's obvious the locket is yours but how did it get to be buried on that grave, and who was the man who led me there?"

"I'd better try and explain then," she began. She opened the clasp at the edge of the locket and it sprung open. "Look at this." She passed it to me and taking it in my hands I could see that on the inside were two portraits, one of a young woman and the other a man. The woman was beautiful, her hair plaited around her head in coils, a jewel hung from each ear. She was wearing a rich

12

gown of green. The man was dark haired and handsome and was also dressed in rich clothes. There was something about him that I recognised - his eyes perhaps, dark and deep-set. Then I realised that it was him - it was the dark-eyed stranger who'd led me to the locket.

"The woman is me, many years ago," she said. "And the man was my love, my dear husband-to-be who alas disappeared before we could wed. People said he'd thought better of it and had run away but I never believed he would do that to me. We loved each other deeply and he'd never have betrayed me like that. My parents disapproved of him and said we couldn't marry so we used to meet secretly under the yew tree in the church yard. He gave me that locket the day before we were due to elope together. It was the only way, we thought, then the next day when I awoke, the locket had gone and so had he. I waited for him under the yew tree but he never appeared. Every day I waited for him, every day for years but he never came back. I gave up in the end. My parents died some years later and I've lived here all alone ever since."

"Such a sad story," I held the locket out to her and she took it back into her hands, smiling to herself as she did so.

She went on. "I never forgot him and never married. He broke my heart." She held the locket by the chain and as she spoke it began spinning, just as it had for me at the grave. It seemed to be pulling her in the direction of the door. I stared, that chill swept across my shoulders again.

"It's telling you something," I whispered. "Perhaps we should go where it leads?"

The locket was moving with more urgency as she stood and made her way to the door. She opened it and stepped outside with me following closely behind. Then it stopped. Nothing. It was completely still. I looked about to see if the dark stranger was there but he was nowhere to be seen. As I turned back to her I noticed a small recess in the wall of the house, only about the size of a small apple. It was covered in cobwebs and dried leaves. I was drawn to the space as I'd been drawn to the grave. I shuddered, unwilling to put my hand into the unknown, wondering briefly if there were a spider's nest in there but had no choice and thrust in my hand, groping about tentatively. I could feel something cloth-like and pulled it out. It was torn and faded, nothing but an old piece of rag.

"Let me see," the woman took the rag from me. "We need some light," she said and went back into the house and sat down beside the fire once more. "Bring the candle closer, there's writing on one side." As she read it out the tears began to fall from her eyes. I had never seen such pain nor heard such a sad tale.

"My dearest,

"I cannot put this letter into your hand, nor speak to you in person. Therefore I am leaving it in a place where I hope you will find it. Your father came to see me this morning and gave me no choice but to leave. He gave me your locket and said that you no longer loved me, that you had chosen to marry another. Is this true? If so, my heart is broken and I will leave this place forever tonight. I have sent a message to you through your sister to tell you to look in our secret place where I have left this letter. I couldn't trust the letter to her hand as I believe all your family are against us but hope that she will at least tell you what I have asked her to.

"I will wait until midnight tonight and if you come, we will be together for ever. If you don't come, I will understand that what your father tells me is the truth and you will never see me again but I will carry your locket with me wherever I go as a memory of our love. Should you come and I am not there, then fear the worst, for your father has threatened me with death.

"I am forever yours,

Roger"

She sat weeping for a long while. I was weeping also, unable to comfort her. Finally she stirred herself, wiping her eyes. "You found this locket on a grave in the church-yard?" she asked. I nodded. "Then he must be dead. So, he did love me. He wouldn't have left my locket there. I think I've always known in my heart that he wasn't alive."

We sat for what seemed like hours, until the dawn light began to change the shape of the room. I was so tired, my eyelids heavy and soon a found myself slipping off to sleep. The old woman didn't seem to notice as I laid down on the hearth to keep warm. I remember vaguely sensing her move about the room and then I heard a door gently open and close. I must have slept half the day away for when I awoke the sun was shining through the windows and was high in the sky. I stirred myself and looked about me. No sign of the woman although lying on the hearth next to me was a box, wooden, with a lock on the lid. I picked up the box, it was small though heavy and I could hear something metal rattling inside. Looking around for the key, I realised that something was hanging from a string around my neck. It was a key and it fit the lock. I opened the box and looked inside. It was filled with gold sovereigns, more than I could ever have dreamed of owning in my whole lifetime. I tipped them out on the floor, excitement mounting as I counted them - fifty sovereigns! A fortune indeed.

I sat for a while, pondering the mystery and decided to look about the house for the woman. I searched every room but there was no sign of her. Finally, I gathered up the sovereigns and once I had carefully locked them back in the box I carried them out of the house and began to make my way back to The Froddington Arms. As I left, however, I felt compelled to look in the secret place again and thrusting in my hand once again, I discovered that there was indeed something else in there. I pulled out a scrap of paper with the words "thank you" written on it. Inside the paper was wrapped the locket. I opened the clasp of the locket to look once more at the portraits but it was empty. The locket glistened in the sunlight and I felt a warm glow inside me whilst I gazed upon it.

Once again in the bridleway outside the wooden gates, I hesitated to go directly to the inn and turned instead towards the church yard. All looked so different in the sunshine but I soon found the yew tree and the grave-stone beneath its boughs. I crouched down to read the name on the grave but it was faded and worn with age. Feeling disappointed that the mystery would remain unsolved I stood up and made to leave. As I looked across in the bright light of day, I swear I could see the shadow of the dark stranger standing there, no longer alone, for next to him was a beautiful young woman with her hair plaited about her head, and they were both smiling at me.

Before leaving I felt obliged to return first to the Froddington Arms to pay for my lodgings but as I approached the inn I realised that it was just a shell of a building, neglected and empty. I slipped the locket's chain over my head and began the long walk home, my night in Froddington a mystery I've never been able to fully fathom. Needless to say though, the farm was saved and we have had many a fruitful year's harvests since.

The Picture

Gran's house was small and dark. Once inside the front door, there you were, in the sitting room crammed with furniture. A red chenille-draped table almost filling the room competed with the ornate fireplace, its mantle piece laden with brass curiosities brought back from India by Uncle Jack.

Gran sat on an old horse-hair stuffed sofa at the far end of the room, which wasn't very far, there only being room for her short legs to stretch out before her without kicking the dining chairs which were pushed tightly under the table. Passing round the table, young children were wary of what lurked beneath the mysterious drapes of blood-red chenille. Sometimes the malicious claws of Gran's cat flashed out to catch them unawares.

Gran would sit regally on her sofa, receiving family members like a Grand Duchess. Sometimes she would reach up to a jar from the shelf beside her and offer any small child in the vicinity a mouth-watering toffee to chew. Many a time, whilst sitting on the hearth rug, my mind would drift away from Gran's talk to the family portrait on the wall behind her. I would study the faces of my long-dead relatives, imagining their lives, their dreams, and where and how they lived. I spent so much time gazing at this picture, that it is ingrained in my memory. I would know it anywhere, even fifty years on.

It was a wet November day that I was hurrying through the rain to the car park, when I paused in front of a shop window. There was the picture of Gran and her family, gazing at me with ageless eyes, accusing me of abandoning them to this life in a dusty, damp, shop window.

As soon as I arrived home, I unwrapped my parcel with care and gently placed it on top of the dresser. The picture was dated 15th November, 1904. Memories of Gran and her tiny cluttered house came flooding back. I could smell the mustiness and even taste the creamy toffee offering in my mouth. I studied the faces in the photograph. Four children sat in front of Gran - three girls in smocks, their long hair be-ribboned. The one boy was dressed in breeches, wool socks and boots. Gran sat on the sofa next to Auntie Flo with Great Granddad standing behind them all. Uncle Jack was to the left of the group, his hand resting on the back of the sofa.

I shrugged myself back to the present and went through to the kitchen to make some tea. Sitting at the kitchen table, the picture kept flashing into my mind's eye. I took my tea into the sitting room and sat looking again at the faces staring out into eternity. There they all were, the same as ever, except, how strange, Uncle Jack somehow seemed less defined than the rest. I held the picture up to the light, thinking that perhaps it was the dark corner of the room to blame. But no, the rest of the picture was clear - it was just Uncle Jack who seemed paler than the rest. I shivered, then replacing the photograph on the dresser, went back into the kitchen and started crashing pots and pans about in preparation for dinner. By the time Alan was home, I had convinced myself that it was definitely my imagination. I was quite excited about my find though and started telling him about it. As soon as we'd eaten, Alan went into the sitting room to look at the picture whilst I cleared away the dishes. He was sitting with it on his lap when I joined him.

"What do you think?" I asked, "What about Uncle Jack in his uniform, eh? He was in the Infantry in India."

Alan looked across the room at me, and I knew that look. "Which one's Uncle Jack?"

"The soldier," I replied. "The one on the left, standing with his hand resting on the sofa."

Alan looked at the picture, then back at me. He slowly turned the picture round. I crossed the room for a closer look. I could see Uncle Jack, but only the faint outline of his body. He was so faint that I would not have seen him at all had I not known that he was there.

"I swear, Alan, that Uncle Jack was in that photograph. He was an Infantryman in India."

Alan, never one to believe anything that wasn't in black and white in front of his face, glazed over and said "Whatever", whilst picking up the newspaper. He slipped into another universe of interesting facts and fiction and left me alone in mine.

Determined to get to the bottom of this, I sat trying to recall some of the stories I'd heard Gran tell and I remembered a box that Gran had left me. It was probably an hour later that I found what I was looking for. In the bottom

19

of the box, amongst dusty photographs of my mother as a little girl, was a small brown notebook with the name Jack Parker carefully inscribed on the cover.

My feelings on opening the notebook are hard to describe. I sat poring over the notes written inside as Uncle Jack's life in India came alive. Each page was filled with the richness of a world I had only seen on film, the searing heat, the colours, the vast range of tastes and smells, all were here in these pages, together with accounts of life in the barracks and on patrol across the lush landscapes at a time of British Imperialism. He told of terrorism which was starting to break out in Bengal, of the dangers in just walking the streets outside the barracks and the restlessness of the local people.

I turned to the next page. It was blank, as was the rest of the notebook. As I flicked through the pages a slip of paper fell to the floor. I picked it up and glancing at it, read the following:

"It is with regret that I have to inform you that Infantryman Jack Parker was killed in action on 15th November, 1904."

The Fancy Dress Party

Tom knew it was serious when he realised that the sex was not enough any more. It was all very well screwing your best friend's wife, but once the initial excitement had worn off, you either knocked it on the head and moved on, or you took it one step further. So, here he was, waiting for Carole to turn up. She had sworn undying love to him and the plan was to pack up everything and leave town together.

By eight o'clock, Tom was getting jittery. Not quite cold feet, but definitely starting to see the other side of the story. By eight-thirty he'd convinced himself that she wasn't going to show and his first thought was that he'd had a lucky escape. Then, as he drove away, the worms in his belly started eating away at him, stirring up those feelings of resentment towards Carole, jealousy towards Paul, and bitterness towards them both. By the time he got home he'd formed half a plan. It was only half a plan, without really meaning to take it all the way.

It was Paul's birthday. Tom had left the invitation on the mantle-piece.

"Fancy Dress!" He snorted at the mirror.

Too late to go out shopping, but there was that trunk in the spare room, left behind by one of his many past conquests. Tom realised he had hit the jackpot as he pulled out the red silk Mandarin's robe from the trunk. Underneath, solemnly gazing at him was a grotesque, morose mask, decorated in gold, the mouth a red, gaping grimace of hatred and fear.

Hurriedly donning the gown, Tom took up the mask. There beneath it was the dagger. He turned it over in his hands, examining the jewel-encrusted hilt, the fine, curved blade, glinting in the light.

Tom shuddered a little, shook his head, placed the dagger back in its place in the trunk and, snatching up the mask without a second thought, he put it on and left the house with a crash of the front door.

Although Paul's house was only a short walk away, Tom soon realised the folly of walking the streets in full fancy dress. Sniggers turned to looks of alarm as people hurried past. This only made Tom stronger, filling him with a mysterious powerful feeling.

The door was already open when he arrived. Sweeping in, but still unsure of his plan, he pushed through a throng of vicars and tarts, fairies and pirates, searching for Carole. The crowd parted, the happiness on their faces faded into looks of horror as each person turned to look at him. Tom felt the resentment growing inside as he passed through, determined to get back to them later, but now, he had more important issues to deal with.

The party spilled out into the lamp-lit garden and Tom found himself drawn out onto the lawn. The lights were Chinese lanterns which seemed to lead him down the path the the summer house. Fashioned in the style of a Chinese pagoda, its many tiers were decorated with oriental lions and dragons gazing down at Tom as he moved closer to his fate.

Tom froze as, glancing up at the window, he saw the silhouette of two people entwined in each other's arms. Paul and Carole! Together, laughing softly, that intimate laughter of lovers sharing a moment no other could share.

The soft moan from Tom's lips startled them out of their intimacy. They turned as one in his direction, a faintly puzzled look on Carole's face as she half-recognised the familiar noise. Paul was smiling, the smile of the host greeting a guest.

Tom knew deep down that this was the moment when he should have cut his losses and left, or maybe tried his luck elsewhere with one of the many other willing women inside the house who were flaunting their bodies to anyone who cared to look.

He just stood there, rooted to the spot, while Carole and Paul's mutual happiness turned to fear. A feeling of power, a burning desire for revenge was sweeping over Tom as Paul moved towards him down the steps of the summer house. As Paul opened his mouth to speak, Tom's arm thrashed out to push him away. The jewels on the dagger's hilt glinted in the lantern light as Tom thrust it deep into Paul's heart. Paul sank slowly to the ground at Tom's feet.

Tom stared in horror at the dagger still in his hand, Paul's blood dripping from the blade. He looked up at Carole who was frozen in fear at the top of the steps.

Tom could not speak. He tried to remember what had happened before he left his house, and knew that he had definitely left the dagger safely in the trunk, but here it was, in his hand. He tried to turn and run, but his feet seemed to be stuck as if in a boggy mire. He tried to throw the dagger away into the bushes, but his arms were numb. He found his legs taking him towards Carole, slowly, step by step. He tried to call out to her, to warn her, but no words would form in his mouth, only a deep moaning sound which came from the depths of his soul. He wanted to take off the mask, to trample it under his feet, but he knew he was truly in its power.

Reaching Carole, he gently placed his free hand against her cheek in a last hopeless gesture of tenderness, looked deep into her eyes, then, very carefully, pushed the dagger almost gently into her heart.

The Bride of the Sea

The mermaid sat upon the rock dreaming about what life would be like on the shores beside the sea. Her mind drifted with the waves washing onto the sand, into dreams far beyond her experience.

On this particular evening, whilst her mind was far away, she was awoken from her reverie by a handsome young mortal. It would have been better had he not seen her, but once he'd set eyes on her, she knew that he would be entranced, for this was the way of things. It was easy for her to be drawn into the mood of the moment, being wooed by such a man. He seemed so much more exciting than the mermen of her watery home.

Before much time had passed, he was begging her to stay ashore with him and to marry him. The mermaid knew in her heart that this was the wrong thing to do, that the two worlds could not live long together in harmony, but something drew her on. She wanted to say yes. Her curiosity of what life as a human woman would be like was overwhelming, but the thought of spending the rest of her life out of the ocean was too much to bear. She thought about this for some time, gazing out across the sea, whilst the young man waited impatiently for her answer.

Gradually, an idea began to take shape in her mind. She would make a condition of her marriage that should the man strike her three times, then he would lose her and she would return to the ocean forever. She knew that he would find it impossible never hit out at her, even if it was only in jest. That would ensure her way of escape. She told the young man that she would marry him, would bring him riches, that she would bear him a beautiful child, and be a good wife to him. The young man was delighted. Then the mermaid gave him the condition of the marriage, that if he should strike her three times, then she would leave him and return to the sea forever.

The young man, thinking that the condition was an easy one to keep as he was in the first flush of young love, readily agreed. They were duly married, and the mermaid indeed kept her promise. She brought riches from the sea to the marriage and was a good and faithful wife. She revelled in living above the waves and spent much time with her new husband, learning to run on the sands, gather flowers in the meadows, and enjoyed the pleasure of sitting beside a log fire in winter. In due course of time, she bore a son, a beautiful child, as she had foretold before her marriage. Her life was perfect. She had long ago stopped thinking about living beneath the sea, she was so happy with her new family.

One day on a hot, sunny afternoon, the young couple were sitting in the garden, watching their child play on the grass. Bees were buzzing and birds were singing in the trees. The mermaid found herself slipping into a peaceful, dreamy sleep. Her husband looked down at her fondly, feeling so much love in his heart for her. As he watched, he noticed a bluebottle alight on her arm, and he gently flicked it away with the palm of his hand. At once, she awoke from her dream, a look of fear in her eyes. "You struck me!" she said. "That is once, only two left!" Until he had struck her she had forgotten the condition she had imposed on him. The feeling of panic fluttered in her breast.

From that day forward, something seemed to be lacking in their world, a cloud had formed on the horizon and nothing, not even the tinkling laughter of their child's voice, could make things as they were. Oh, how the mermaid wished that she had not been so hasty in making the condition to their marriage! She was always on edge, creeping around as if on eggshells, not wanting to upset her man, just in case he should forget and strike her again. Gradually, day by day, week by week, the time slipped by, the cloud forming in the distance seemed to be coming nearer and nearer, and nothing seemed to be able to stop its coming.

"I must stop thinking this way," the mermaid told herself, "and just enjoy life as it is."

She tried hard to regain the same happiness she felt before and each time the thought came back to her, she pushed it away and turned her mind to something else. The child grew strong and the mermaid was proud of him. He spent time with his father, fishing on the shore, working in the fields, and returned home each evening with fish to eat, or vegetables from the earth. During the long winter nights, they spent time by the fire, singing and telling tales. Sometimes they would play games by the firelight. The man taught the boy how to play draughts, and the mermaid would sit and watch. She felt happier but still the shadow was clouding her life, like a ticking clock, waiting for time to run out.

One evening such as this, sitting beside the fire, watching her son and husband play, the mermaid was making a woollen coat for her son. As she worked, the ball of wool rolled from her lap and into the fireplace. She leaned forward to pick it up and the chair beneath her gave way. She felt herself slipping forward into the fire. Swiftly, her husband struck his arm forward to catch her, accidentally flicking the back of his hand onto her shoulder as he did so.

"That's twice!" she screamed, and she burst into loud sobbing. She cried and cried all night, completely inconsolable. Her husband could do nothing to make her feel any better, although he tried to assure her that he would never hurt her.

After a long and sleepless night, the mermaid had made up her mind that there was only one way to resolve this terrible spell she had cast on her happiness. She would have to return to the sea, seek out her father and ask his help in reversing the condition she had placed on her marriage agreement. As soon as her husband had left for the day's fishing, taking their young son with him, the mermaid searched in her trunk for the mermaid skin she had hidden there so long ago, and ran down to the sea-shore, slipped on her tail and plunged into the sea. She took one last look at the rocks and the sky, before diving deep into the ocean.

How cool and soothing the green ocean felt to her after such a long time ashore. She delighted in the gentle sound of the sea and the rhythm of the current, pulling her down, down, down, into the depths, as memories of her childhood came rushing into her mind once again. She swam around the beautiful under-seascape, the lovely bright pinks and oranges of the sea anemones, through the shoals of colourful fishes, who blinked their fish-eyes at her as she flew through the waters towards her father's home, deep in a cave near the ocean floor.

Imagine her father's joy at seeing his beautiful daughter again after such a long time. He could hardly believe that it was really she. Only there was a change, she was a mother now, and held the bearing of a wife of the lands rather than of the sea. Father and daughter embraced and cried many tears of both happiness and regret at the passing of the years. Her father looked old and the strain of the years were showing on his face and in the stoop of his shoulders. His tail was slower in its swishing, and his eyes were distant and hurt.

The mermaid sat at his side and told her tale. Such a strange story to the ears of her father, although he had heard in the distant past of young mermaids straying to the surface and becoming mortal wives.

"We were told they were just mythical tales," he said, "but I always had a fear of such a thing happening to my child. That is why I always warned you not to stray on to the lands."

He was so happy that she was back and vowed not to let her out of his sight again.

"But, father," she explained, "I have only returned so that you can help me. I love my mortal husband dearly, and my son, and although when I married him, I believed that it would not last, I now regret that belief and want to stay beside him as his wife for the rest of my life." She then explained to her father of the conditions she had placed upon him when she married the man, and of the two times that he had accidentally struck her.

Her father was devastated at the thought of losing her again and spent many hours trying to persuade her to stay beneath the sea. He eventually agreed to help her but asked that she stay for just three days so that he may get to know her again and have happy memories of her before his life was over. The mermaid was torn between wanting to spend time with her father and the need to return to her husband who had no idea where she had gone. She agreed to stay as she had no real choice if she wanted her father to help her.

Each day was filled with parties, and many mermen and maids came to call, all excited at the sight of the mermaid who had been wed to a mortal. They all gathered around her, all begging her to tell them all she had seen and done.

Each evening, her father sat with her and talked to her of her heritage under the sea. He showed her the riches that would have been hers should she have stayed. Gold and silks from wrecked ships that had sunk off the shores of the land, the very same land where the mermaid had been living, colourful shells and rocks that lit up the cave, beautiful prancing sea horses, sea weeds and corals. The mermaid was sorely tempted to stay and to make her father happy, but on the evening of the third day, she found a mirror and looking into the image of her face, she saw the sadness in her eyes reflecting back at her and realised that she would have to insist on her father's help now, or she would not be able to leave all this again.

She went to her father and begged him to help her break the spell.

"Daughter," he spoke slowly, as if it were a great strain, "You must know, that you have the power to break the spell. It is something you created with your mind and your heart, and you must now search yourself for the remedy."

The mermaid pondered on this for a while, then she realised what her father said was true. She had created the conditions and only her strong belief in them gave them the power they had upon her, and only she had the power to end the belief. She searched in her heart and saw that her love for her mortal husband was stronger than the spell. She would return to the surface lands, and live happily with her husband, never having to return to the sea unless she wanted to.

She embraced her father warmly. "Thank you so much for your wisdom, father," she said. "I will return to my husband and son, but you have helped me see that it need not be a parting from you forever."

"Then you will return and visit me?" her father asked.

"Many times," she replied, "And I will bring my son to the seashore every day to show him the sea. If you should be watching, you may see him, if only from a distance."

"That would make me very happy," he said.

The mermaid took her leave from her father the next morning and swam the long journey back to her home on the shores. She was very tired when she arrived on the land, and spent some time resting on the rocks before taking off her mermaid tail. She began walking up the beach, then, feeling the excitement in her breast at the thought of seeing her beloved husband again, she broke into a run, calling his name as she went.

As she reached the cottage gate she noticed that the flowers in the garden were drooping, the petals were dried and shrivelled. "He has forgotten to water the garden," she thought fleetingly. "I'll soon have it fresh and beautiful again".

Before she could reach the door, it swung open and out stepped a tall, young man. The mermaid was confused. The young man looked so much like both her son and her husband, but surely he could not be either, being too old to be her son and far too young to be her husband.

"Mother?" As soon as he had spoken she knew it had to be her son, although she could not understand how he could have grown up so quickly in just three days. The she remembered, with a sinking heart that each day under the ocean was three years on the land. She had been away for nine years! How could she have forgotten?

"My son," she cried. "What have I done? Where is your Father?'

"When you left us," he began, "Father was broken hearted. He stood on the shore day after long day, staring out to sea. Whatever I said or did to distract him, made no difference. He would not speak, nor eat, nor sleep. Weeks passed, then one morning I went to find him but he had gone. All I could find was a note on a rock telling me that he could not live on the land without his one true love so he had gone into the sea to be with you."

The mermaid turned and walked back to the shore. Her heart was heavy as she gazed out to sea, knowing deep inside that she would never see her love again. She took one last look at the land before she strode into the sea, leaving her tail on the shore. The waters covered her head and soon there was nothing left to see but the ocean, gleaming in the sunlight.

The Box

Trudging to the bottom of the garden, clutching close to my chest the shoe box, tears seemed to be leaking from my eyes. I wiped my nose on my sleeve. My feet and my heart were heavier with each step until at last I stopped at the apple tree, took a deep breath, and placed the box carefully on the ground. The hole was small, too small for the memories of a life so big and so beautiful, yet the box was small too. "Get a grip woman," I said out loud. "It's only a cat."

But it wasn't only the cat being dead that was killing me, ripping open the raw wounds. It was the memories of how good life had been when we'd first got the dear little thing, and how easily it had all slipped away.

HE had said he hated cats, but we'd laughed together as she ran up the apple tree and got stuck at the top of the fragile branch that had swayed to and fro with the weight of her, and she'd never seemed to learn as it happened time after time.

"Get on with it." The order came in HIS voice.

I picked the small box up and gently placed it in the grave. "Goodbye, dear friend," I gulped back lumps of sorrow which were filling my throat like vomit.

I picked up the garden spade and began to cover the box with the newly dug earth.

"What are you doing that for?" HIS voice was loud. I spun around to see where he was.

"I'm burying Jess. She got run over."

I couldn't see HIM, but he must have been hiding behind the Rowan tree which was in the middle of the garden and was pretty overgrown.

"You always were stupid." HIS voice was clear. "I can't believe you're burying the cat in the garden."

I tried to ignore his voice as I filled the hole that I'd so carefully dug, the soft earth soon covering the box. HIS presence was still there, behind my left shoulder somewhere. I tried to ignore it.

"Please, dear angels, take care of her," I took up the spade and walked back to the house, unlocked the door and went in.

Something brushed past my shoulder as I entered the kitchen, sending a shiver through me. I tried to shake off the feeling that there was someone else in the house with me, a feeling I'd had frequently since he'd gone.

The door safely locked, I relaxed. It was strange though, how empty the house seemed without HIM there. It had been so full before, his personal items draped around me like curtains. It had taken days to pack everything up after he had gone, days filled with remorse, anger, and something else. It might have been elation, but I couldn't remember what that had felt like. And then, yesterday as all his things were taken away, such a feeling of relief. I had to celebrate somehow.

So I'd gone out last night. Not with anyone. There are no friends left to celebrate with, HE had made sure of that. But I'd gone out and just drove around. I'd sat looking at the sea, at the metal grey ocean crashing against the shingle, sucking down the loose stones into its depths, just as my future was dragging me screaming out of my past.

I drove home again feeling renewed and went from room to room in the house, searching for something which was no longer there. I'd made sure that there was nothing left to remind me. But there were shadows in the mirrors and glimpses of memories out of the corner of my eyes which became more real as the evening passed.

Lying on the bed, I thought I heard him coming up the stairs, could even hear his breathing in the hall, but when I got up to look, the hall was just an empty space. I couldn't relax. Relaxation was not for me yet. Not until I was completely sure that he would never come back into this house, or indeed, into my life again.

I crept down the stairs into the hall and stood for a while by the front door. Below my feet was the trap-door to the cellar, covered by an old brown rug. I took a deep breath, rolled back the rug and pulled open the air-tight door. The stench reached me out of the darkness, sucking me in as the waves on the shore had dragged down the shingle. I reached for the light switch, flicked it on with my outstretched hand. Light flooded the damp room revealing the shelves of wine bottles, carefully stacked against the far wall. My eyes were watering. I covered my nose and mouth with my hand, and braced myself to peer into the darkness of the recess under the arched stone wall. Just to be sure.

HE was still there, sitting where I'd left him, his legs

hanging over the end of the box, his blood congealed and black in his sandy hair. I stood over him, the feeling of relief broken by the sound of knocking at the front door.

"Got to go now and answer the door," I said, flicking off the light as I climbed the steps. The trap-door shut with a bang and I carefully rolled the rug back into place. I took up a bottle of Chanel from the hall table, sprayed perfume around the hall and opened the door with a smile.

Out of Little Things

When you gave me that acorn and said, so romantically, "Out of little acorns, great things grow," I thought you were talking about our relationship. You know, that you were growing to love me and things could only get better and all those other awful cliches.

I remember that day so clearly - do you? How we walked along the shingle beach, stumbling. You caught me as I fell from the breakwater, still slippery from the past night's frost. You held me close, so close that I could feel the mist from your mouth as you laughed. You held me for just a little longer than you needed to and our eyes were caught in the moment, just one brief flash of time, on repeat ever since in my memory.

The acorn grew hot in my hand as we walked to the pier. I clung to it like a limpet to a rock as I dreamed of a future with you - you as my rock, always there when I needed someone to cling to. You made me feel safe, needed. We were in rhythm with each other for that moment and when the waves crashed in too far, you lifted me up to save my feet from getting salty wet. We laughed.

The pier was empty and no wonder - but the hole in the fence let us in. "It'll be fun," you said as you dragged me through the gap, too small to save my scarf from catching on the torn edge. I tried to pull it free and felt the sharp scratch on the back of my hand. A trickle of blood was a small river that dripped onto the wooden planks until you took my hand in your mouth, licking the blood with your hot tongue. You looked at me and I felt my stomach churn as I saw your blood-stained teeth smiling at me.

"I thought we were going for fish and chips," I said, but you wanted danger first. We walked past the old worn ballroom, the ghosts of sixties bands screaming into the winter winds through the broken windows. Then on past the vacant bolts which once held roundabouts and candy-floss stands, you said we should go right to the end where the Victorian railings were rusty and worn. I wondered how they'd survived the war. You leaned over and I cried out in alarm - I could see the folly of it all. You beckoned me on.

Still holding tightly to the acorn in my hand, I succumbed to your goading me to climb onto the top rail. I felt the metal creaking under my weight and saw the glint in your eye when you realised I was going to fall. Of course, you caught me in time .... that time.

The cafe was open at the far end of the promenade - the coffee was a welcome relief. I winced as I burnt my tongue. Your laughter turned to mockery and I looked away from you. We were the only customers that day, alone and lonely in a room of cold draughts and steam, now silently fighting against each other.

The fish and chips arrived, disappointed like a deflated balloon, flat on a plate, the red of the ketchup on yours, flashing at me across the table a warning signal which I didn't take. I was in love. I slipped my hand into my pocket and felt the acorn there, still warm from my hand.

Through my window now, I watch the birds on the feeder which hangs from the oak tree and think back again and again to that day. I try not to think about the later ones. The sun is hidden behind a grey sheet which lays over the gardens and rooftops all around. There's not much of a view here. Just the oak tree which neighbours say blocks the light to their windows. I wonder whether it's time to chop the bloody thing down. After all, it's served its purpose and the neighbours would be much happier. I could put the bird feeder on a post and sit under an umbrella for shade. I don't need the tree any more.

I put on my coat and walk to the sea. I need to think away from the house, away from the tree. I walk past the pier - the lights are bright and there are people bustling through the door into the arcade - loud music shouts onto the promenade, mingled with laughter. Children eat ice-cream in the chill of the afternoon just because they can. It's the seaside, after all. I mourn the loss of the children we never had and start to walk back to the house.

At the door, I hesitate, as I always have, calming my breathing, settling the knives in my stomach, soothing them into softness even though I know I don't need to feel this any more. I turn the key in the lock and push the door open, every movement, every sound as I move through the house, is new. The past is over. Just one more thing to do. The back door is still ajar - I know I left it open when I went out. Now I feel strong enough to step out into the garden.

I walk to the tree, look at the ground and find a newly fallen acorn. I slip it into my pocket and smile. I look up and feel happy inside.

You're still there, swinging a bit in the breeze, the birds still enjoying the feast of fresh meat.

Bearskin

It is white in the land and cold. The forest is dark and all the gentle animals are either hiding in caves, or deep under the ground, where all God-fearing creatures should be. In the village of Milton, the people stay hidden, too, warm and safe beside their fires, only ever scurrying out when there is no choice, to find more wood, or perhaps to creep into the edge of the dark, treacherous forest to hunt for a morsel of meat to fill their hollow bellies.

It was the boy's turn to do his duty by his Grandfather who lived alone in the deepest part of the forest, only ventured to in the Spring and Summer, unless the bitter months drew out, as they were this long, long winter. The wind howled around the chimneys as the boy wound his bear-skin cloak around his lithe and innocent form. He carefully wrapped the still-warm, freshly baked loaves of bread in the blood red cloth his mother had given him, and placed the parcel in his satchel, together with the small cask of wine, essential foodstuffs to ward off the bitter winter's chill.

Before he began his journey, the boy's mother handed him the long bladed knife once used for skinning the great Black Bear whose hide he wore. The boy slipped the knife into its sheath and embracing his mother, turned and left the cottage to begin his journey through the pure white landscape to his Grandfather's house.

The forest became quieter and quieter as he trudged. No sound, not even his footsteps broke the virginal membrane of silence in his ears. He had walked for perhaps an hour when he saw the girl. She came from nowhere. One moment he looked up from the snow in front of his feet and she was there. He had noticed no footprints, just the eternally smooth, white blanket covering the land.

The girl was naked, her jet black hair falling in seductive ripples the length of her mottled blue and white-skinned back, her body swaying with the rhythm of her stride as she walked just ahead of him. As she turned to look at him, he caught a glimpse of her nipples, erect with the cold. A flood of emotions rushed through the boy's body. He had never seen a woman naked before. It didn't occur to him how cold she must be as he felt the heat of desire pumping through his veins. He just knew that he had to have her, to touch her skin, to caress her hair, to feel her nakedness against his own young body. He called out to her and she turned again and smiled. How red were her lips, full of the promise he had never experienced. She was moving too fast as he broke into a run, realising fleetingly but not caring that the familiar part of the forest was long ago left behind.

At last in a clearing she stopped and turned to him, opening her arms with a welcoming look in her eye. He was entranced with the beauty of her nakedness, her black hair flowing over the curves of her breasts, her nipples inviting him, the same blood red of her lips in contrast to the whiteness of her skin. He drank greedily of the sight. Before he had taken more than a step towards her, he saw that there were other women there, almost blinding him with their voluptuous bodies. He longed to touch them, to feel and taste them but they were always tantalizingly just beyond his reach. At times he was close enough to smell the muskiness of their bodies and he knew that they desired him just as much as he wanted them.

In my frantic dance, I notice the bread tumble out from my satchel, still half wrapped in the blood red cloth. As it lands in the snow, some of the women break away from the dance, and ripping the cloth, devour the bread in a frenzy of hunger sated at last. The wine cask falls too, crashing to the ground, the soft snow breaking its fall, the stopper bursts forth and the wine bleeds into the pure white snow, the stain spreading ever outwards.

The first girl is taking my hand, guiding me to the centre of the clearing. I see nothing now but her perfect body, knowing that I will soon be fulfilled. I feel hands gently undressing me, caressing me into a state of full arousal as my Beauty lies on the altar, her hair flowing down like black water to the snow-covered ground, her legs long and inviting, her thighs white and firm as she lies willing me on to lie with her. I am helped on to the altar and can wait no longer. I cannot even see the women surrounding us, my eyes are blind to anything but desire.

A knife flashes and a roar fills my ears. The pure skin of the girl becomes mottled. Hair - no! Rough fur is growing across her perfect breasts. Her face is changing, blurring. Her seductive lips draw back to reveal drooling teeth and tongue, her tiny nose thrust forth into a wet, black snout. The arms around me grow stronger now, her claws tear into my back. As I arch in pain and ecstasy the bear-skin cloak which was so carefully taken from me earlier is once again wrapped around my form. As I reach the inevitable climax and my seed bursts forth into the willing belly of the Beauty, I realise I am fusing with a Great Black Bear. Part of my mind is fighting against this, recoiling in horror, but I know deep inside myself that I am fulfilling a terrible destiny.

Still, I try to break away. Wildly looking around the clearing, I see the women have all gone. There is just myself and my terrible bride.

I raise myself up on my rear legs and roar from the depths of my soul.

Portsea Basin

It was just before dawn on a damp November morning. Joe walked home after a long and difficult night shift. Normally he loved the walk home in the dark. It gave him a chance to leave behind his work and prepare for the day ahead - a couple of hours sleep and then off to his job in the Charlotte Street market. As he turned into Arundel Street, just a few more yards to his flat, he felt a change in the air. A mist was swirling about the trees, newly planted in the precinct. He walked a little faster and nearly fell over the man sitting on the bench in the middle of the street. Joe stopped just in time.

"Sorry. I didn't see you there." He looked down at the man. He hadn't even flinched. "Are you alright?" Joe asked. No answer came. He could see the man was awake but he didn't even look up at him. Joe shrugged and walked on. He hadn't gone more than a few steps when he heard the sound - the sound of a heavy horse's hooves on cobbles, water lapping in the background. He turned back to look and the man had gone. The sounds had gone. All that remained was the drip, drip, drip of the rain from the roof overhanging the shops.

If they hadn't dredged the canal it may have been different. I'd been lying there for months, the fishes nibbling at my flesh, water snails sliding between my toes, my body weighted by the rocks tied around my waist with ropes still yet to rot. You thought I'd abandoned you but I never would have done that. I was waiting for you, waiting at the canal basin, waiting as we'd agreed the night before.

The day was nearly over, the evening sun glowed red on the still water. All seemed at peace. The barge would be leaving in an hour, our passage booked to London. We knew that this was the safest way to get you away - the road to London would have been the first place they'd have looked once they'd discovered you missing.

Looking back now, I wish that I'd been stronger, that I'd not delayed and had agreed to leave when you'd first told me about the child. If only I hadn't hesitated.

As the dirty waters were pumped from the muddy basin and I looked down on my mouldering body, I was glad you weren't there to see what was left of me. I wondered where you were - I wondered about our child. I was so busy wondering about things that I hadn't noticed him standing there on the bank. His face was like a thunderstorm, ready to burst forth. He was also looking down at my body. I stood behind him, wanting to push him over the edge into the murky slime but the past weeks and months had taught me the impossibility of this, my own body being of no further use to me. Had I tried to push him, my hand would have gone straight through his body and the worst he would have felt was a shiver of someone walking over his grave.

I watched, helpless, as he looked about, and seeing that he was completely alone and safe from the prying eyes of the living, he made his way to a nearby stack of timber and began to carry a log back to the bank. He dropped the log onto my poor half-eaten body. The mud was soft beneath my remains and as the log hit my chest I sank a little. It may have been my imagination but I swear I felt a thud as it landed. Still my body could be seen from the bank. He fetched another log, then another and another, dropping each one onto my body until it was completely covered. I felt the dull echo of pain as each one dropped, sensing the vitriol from the man on the bank - the man who'd been your cruel suitor, the man who had murdered me.

No doubt he'd been confident that the canal waters would hide his crime but the contamination of the City's wells put paid to that. When the local people began to complain of the salt water which was seeping through from the canal, tainting the once-fresh waters, the engineers decided that it should be dredged. That was when my body saw the light of day once more.

Now, my remains again out of sight, the evil man smiled down at the mud and laughed. He laughed and walked away. I tried to follow him, to find where you were, to somehow let you know that I hadn't abandoned you by choice but I found that I could only stay within the confines of the canal basin.

Frustrated, I waited. I wondered if you would come this way again and that I could see you one more time before I left this Earthly domain. I could never be at peace with you not knowing. You never came. But he did. He came back, over and over again, stood on the bank of the canal and looked down at where I lay, almost as if he was waiting for me to rise up and show myself to him. I wished that I could have but it was out of my power to do so.

Then, one night, after dusk, he appeared at the end of the alleyway, standing in the shadows, looking around to see if the coast was clear. There was no-one about, only me, as ever, waiting and watching. The canal had long been filled again with water, the work all finished and the wells once more flowing with clear, sweet waters. Several narrow boats and a couple of barges were tethered along the banks, the horses grazing in the meadow just beyond the basin. In the distance, voices and laughter could be heard from a local hostelry as the owners of the boats unwound after a long day on the canal. But there was no one to be seen on the banks of the basin.

I watched as he crept from the darkness of the alley and made his way to the edge of the waters. Then I noticed that he held a bundle in his arms. A bundle which was moving and as I watched I heard the sound of a baby cry. I looked on in horror as he picked up an empty sack which had been discarded on the bank. He selected a number of heavy-looking stones and placed them in the sack. Then, more awful still, he bundled the child into the sack also, tying a string around its neck before he slung it into the middle of the canal basin and then stood watching as the bag sank out of sight. My child! Murdered!

This was too much for me - I summoned up all of the anger I could feel for the loss of our child, the loss of you, the loss of my young life, and willed him to topple over the edge. I saw him trying to resist. He struggled but I was stronger. He swayed, a look of fear and shock on his face as he realised that he was falling forward, in slow motion, into the deepest part of the canal basin. As he landed, I heard his head strike something in the depths. It was one of the logs he'd used to cover my body. Simultaneously, I felt him falling onto my rotting body. Unhappily for him, striking the log rendered him unconscious. He would have floated up to the surface if his belt hadn't caught onto my skeletal hand which had somehow become uncovered. I felt my dead fingers entwine around the strap.

On the bank, my ghostly self watched and smiled as his breath bubbled to the surface and I stood there, staring into the water long after the bubbles had ceased.

Many years have passed and still I remain here, unable to leave the basin, waiting in vain for a glimpse of you, long after your life must have ended. I never saw you again. I don't suppose I'll ever be free to rest my soul in peace. Even now, now that the canal is long gone, smooth paving stones taking the place of the waters, I remain here and can still hear the echoes of horse's hooves on stone, the lap the the dirty waters against the barges as if they still moved along the canal. Some mornings I sit and watch as workers make their way home after a night shift. I wonder when I see them, wonder if they can see me, wonder if they are somehow connected to you, wonder whatever happened to you all that time ago.

It was just before dawn on another misty morning in November. Joe walked home from his night shift. No longer alone, he walked with Anna, their heads close together, huddled against the cold morning. Anna stopped suddenly and looked at Joe. 'Did you hear that?' she asked.

'Horses' hooves,' Joe said. 'I've heard it before.'

'And the sound of water lapping against boats. There used to be a canal here, you know. My Great Grandmother used to talk about the canal that went from London to Portsmouth. It passed through Arundel and Chichester apparently. There was talk in our family of a love affair between her and a young man. They were going to elope together - but it never came to anything - they were going to meet here at the canal basin and run away to London.'

'What happened? Did she not go to meet him?'

'She did, but he never turned up. She waited for him but he didn't appear. She married my Great Grandfather in the end.' She shivered. 'He was always a sour-faced man. I don't think they were ever happy.'

Joe and Anna stood in the shelter one of the newly planted trees and listened. The sound of horse's hooves faded into the distance. They still heard the lapping of water, then a sigh. Gradually these sounds faded too, leaving only the drip, drip, drip of water from the balcony of the flats above the shops splashing onto the paving stones where they stood.

One Night in April

I'd been on duty for a couple of hours and was bored. I'd been reading my magazine, passing the time away when I looked up and noticed the Fog had wafted through the doorway and lay like a threadbare carpet in the hallway. There were these two gentlemen standing before the fireplace. One tall, rugged looking, was carrying a stick decorated with a golden crab. He had a distant look in his eye. The other was younger, nervous, his hands restless.

I leaned across the counter, smiled and said a "Good evening," to them.

The younger of the two answered, not a polite "Good Evening" back but a curt "We need two rooms please." The older man stood by the fire, his back turned towards the room.

I tried to make conversation as I passed the register to the young man to sign, asked him if they were here to see the ships.

"What! Oh, no, just some private business," he answered, somewhat hastily I thought.

But I just glanced at his name in the register and said "Very well Mr. Smith. And your companion?" I nodded to the other gentleman by the fire. He was staring into the flickering flames in the fireplace but turned as I raised my voice, "Would you mind, Sir?" His eyes gave me quite a turn - so deep, like the blackness at the bottom of the Harbour. I'd seen that look before in men who'd come into the bar during the war years.

"Of course," he said as he crossed to the counter. As he signed his name I noticed he had a tremor. He gripped the pen tightly as if to rectify his spider-like signature. I took the keys from the hook and offered to show them to their rooms.

Climbing the stairs, they followed closely behind me. I opened the first door in the corridor and stood aside to allow them to see the room. The elder one spoke first. "I'll take this one," he said as he entered the room. He turned to the other. "Meet you in the bar in half an hour, Smith."

The one called Smith nodded saying something like "Very well, Sir." It was more of a bow than a nod as I recall.

The door slammed shut and I was alone in the corridor with him. He was good-looking in a youthful kind of way, reminded me of my little brother who was away at sea. Once away from the older man he seemed more relaxed. He smiled at me and asked me if I would care to join him in a drink later that evening. Of course, I declined politely. "Staff are not allowed to fraternise with the guests Sir," I said.

"Surely one drink would do no harm?"

"Those are the rules, Sir, and the manager watches me like a hawk." I cursed myself for blushing but he did look disappointed as we reached his room. I opened the door and waited whilst he entered, "I hope you will find everything satisfactory, Sir," I said.

I turned on my heels and left the room, feeling no small regret, I can tell you. I stopped outside the elder gentleman's door and listened for a while, wondering what it was about him that was so curious. I've seen many men walk through those hotel doors over the past few years and that harrowing look was so familiar. I heard a chink of a bottle on glass before I moved on to the stairs and hurried back to the reception desk and my magazine.

Later that same evening I was still at my post in the hallway, reading the Evening News. I could see into the smoke-filled bar from where I sat and across the room, sitting in the armchairs beside the fireplace, the same two gentlemen sat, each nursing a large brandy. Their heads bent together seemingly in deep conversation, occasionally glancing around the crowded room as though fearing that they may be overheard. The older gentleman caught my eye as I looked across towards them. I smiled and held his eyes for a moment. His piercing gaze gave me the right shivers so I looked back down at my paper. When I looked up again, he'd turned away. I wondered if I'd imagined it.

I soon put all thought of the two men out of my mind as I read the paper. The front page was full of the news about the goodwill visit by the former leaders of the Soviet Union, Kruschev and Bulganin, who were due to arrive on the cruiser Ordzhonikidze, the following day. I had trouble getting my head and my tongue around how to pronounce that one! The two Soviets were to travel to London by train to meet Mr. Eden. I was so looking forward to seeing Portsmouth full of Soviet sailors. There was sure to be excitement on the streets of the City - such exotic young men, never you mind worrying about communists murdering us in our beds!

I was snapped out of my dreaming when the manager called over to me to get on with clearing some tables in the bar. 'I don't pay you to read the paper,' he grumbled. He did grumble a lot.

I was collecting glasses when I overheard a snippet of conversation from the two gentlemen I mentioned earlier. I wasn't eaves-dropping, just happened to be beside them at the time.

"The weather will be perfect, calm seas and the fog will give you cover," Mr. Smith was saying.

His companion shushed at him and turned to glare at me. When he saw it was me, his mouth forced into a smile but his eyes remained cold and dark. I moved away quickly and began wiping tables across the other side of the room. By the time I'd finished washing up the glasses, the bar had begun to clear and the two men had gone.

I made my way up to my room in the attic, listening outside the older gentleman's door on the way. All was quiet. I lay on my bed, unable to sleep, my mind going over and over the events of the evening. There was something about those two men that I couldn't put my finger on. And what had Mr. Smith meant when he'd said, "the fog will give you cover?"

It was a chilly night for April, the air still not recovered from the coldest March in many years. I had trouble getting warm enough to sleep and was just drifting off in the early hours before dawn, when I thought I heard the sound of footsteps on the stairs. Suddenly I was wide awake. I lay as still as I could, listening hard. I was sure I could hear the sound of breathing outside my door, as if someone was waiting there, listening to me, wondering whether to enter the room. I coughed loudly, hoping to scare off any intruder, then lay still again. My heart was thudding like a bass drum. Finally, not being able to bear it any longer, I threw back the covers and crept across the room. Standing there, listening with one ear to the door, I began to feel a little silly and slowly opened the door. No-one. The hall was empty. I crept back to bed, cold again and lay there trying to sleep. By the time the cathedral clock in the square chimed six, I was up.

I hurried downstairs and put the kettle on before going into the hallway. I looked again at the register and glanced at the names of the two gents: Mr. Bernard Smith and Mr. Lionel Carp. I decided there and then that I wasn't going to worry about those two today, not with all the excitement of the Soviet cruiser due to arrive.

I had the day off and was soon making my way to the Round Tower at the mouth of the Harbour. The crowds were already making their way to the sea-front but I was able to push through to find a position near enough to see the magnificent sight of the cruiser entering Portsmouth - the ship's company lining the decks, the sailors dressed in the kind of uniforms I'd only seen in books about Tsarist Russia, waving and crying to the people, who were returning their cheers with typical Portsmouth enthusiasm. What a wonderful day.

That evening I was back on duty. I noticed that Mr. Smith was dining alone. I stopped at his table and asked if Mr. Carp would be joining him. I swear he blushed as he hesitated and said, "Later perhaps. He has had some family business to deal with."

I was still unsure as to why I was so curious about this man. There was something eerie about him and I had a feeling that something was amiss.

I never did see Mr. Carp again. I thought he must have come in late that evening whilst I was in the kitchen and gone straight up to his room. The next morning, he must have already gone. Mr. Smith collected his belongings, including the stick with the golden crab for a handle. He settled the bill and left.

I got on with my work and the two men soon faded from my memory. There was just one thing - when I came back from the market a few days later, I noticed that a page had been torn from the register. The manager was tight-lipped when I asked him about it. "Least said, soonest mended," was all he said.

Of course, I read the story in the Evening News about the disappearance of Commander Lionel Crabb, who was accused of spying on the Soviet cruiser and when, a year later, a headless body dressed in a frogman's suit was discovered in Chichester Harbour, I went over all cold.

Night Demons

The glint was in your eye long before we met, I dare say. That's what everyone said. The ones I asked, that is. Where to start? Not the beginning - it would take too long.

It was the middle of the night, one of those nights when the darkness is a heavy blanket weighing you down. I was suddenly awake. Breathing in the pitch blackness, I tried to stop my heart beating so that I could listen. My body was too loud, deafening me, filling my ears like the tide flooding into a sinking ship. Every nerve ending in my body screamed at me that something was wrong. The bed felt different, lighter. No stirring beside me. I was alone.

I can't tell whether it was relief I felt, or an even deeper fear, wondering what could have happened. I lay there counting the seconds in my head, waiting for you to return. By the time I had counted twenty minutes away, the sweat breaking out at every sound in the street, every breath of wind in the trees, I decided you weren't coming back. I lay still, trying to think. Maybe I should look downstairs. No, you would be angry if you thought I was monitoring you. Your words. I waited.

I may have drifted off again. No, I was still wide awake, and you hadn't come back. Should I turn the light on? What if you came in and caught me? I wouldn't turn it on just yet. I strained to make my ears listen. I heard the creaking noises of the house, the walls whispering to each other, laughing at me. They knew. It must have been at least an hour later that I gathered the courage to reach out and turn on the light. If you caught me? Don't think it.

The click of the switch was like gunshot. I jumped. Even though it was my hand turning it on, I jumped. Then lay there waiting for the surging in my ears to subside. The silence that followed was less heavy without the darkness folding it into me. Some time passed before I could move again, but eventually I inched my head up to look around the room. I checked your side of the bed, just to be sure. You were definitely not there.

My heart still thudding, and trying to move without disturbing the bed, just in case I was mistaken and you were there after all, somehow hiding under the covers, I slipped out of bed, got dressed and stood in the middle of the room. What would the open door lead to? Escape? Or more of the same? I told myself I had nothing to lose as I turned the handle, gripping it so tightly that my knuckles were bony-white. I pulled the door open and quickly stepped into the hall, closing it behind me. I stood as still as I could. More darkness. No sound.

Now I was really scared. Was I in the house on my own in the dark? I fumbled for the switch on the opposite wall and immediately the hall was flooded with light, no longer a place for fear and phantoms, just the hall of my house, the place I had lived for twenty three years.

The relief was fleeting as I realised I still had to go downstairs. Where would you most likely be? My fear flickered between wanting to find you and wishing my hopes had come to fruition. I had a vague memory but it was unformed, like a dream which slips away into the catacombs of your mind when you waken. Creeping along the hall, holding onto the wall on one side, and the wooden railing of the bannister on the other, I imagined your hands reaching up to grab my ankles and pressed even further away from the railings, just out of your reach.

Then there were the stairs. Looking down into the black well of the hall below, I nearly fainted with the sickness in my stomach, and the pounding in my head. Carefully stepping over that creaking stair, stopping to listen on every step, I clutched at the handrail, the blue veins on my hands standing out hard against my skin.

I saw you. Leaning against the open kitchen doorway, out of the corner of my eye, I could see you, and you were smiling. Not a warm, loving, smile, but one of contempt, that you had caught me out again. The bile rose in my throat. I swung around to face you, but you'd gone.

"You're playing games with me again," I thought. "There's only one way you could have gone without passing me."

But the kitchen was empty, the door to the garden firmly locked and bolted, top and bottom, mocking me in its security. I was trapped. A wave of panic was rising in my chest, my head swam red. I sank to my knees on the kitchen floor, cool and lethal as I knew it would be when my skull cracked against the tiles.

No way out - my strength sapped out of me, my body too heavy to lift. I felt the paralysis creeping through my veins, into every nerve ending. I resigned myself to wait for the inevitable, almost welcoming the end of the nightmare that was my life.

"If I lay down here for a while, it'll be alright." I pressed my face against the comforting cold of the kitchen floor. "Soon it'll be over, soon it'll be over," my mantra for the next eternal moments.

A scream cut through my stupor like a scythe through a meadow, slashing into my senses, urging me back to consciousness and reality. I struggled to move, knowing that I had to get out. There was no choice.

I remembered the telephone on top of the freezer, but it was on the other side of the room and I had to get up off the floor. Perhaps I could just rest for a bit longer? Another scream lashed through me, goading me into action. Something within me forced me up and I found myself holding the phone in my hand, ferociously jabbing at the number pad in sheer panic until I realised that I could not see. I wiped my hand across my eyes and could feel the sticky wet substance on my face. Blood. The reality of it all hit me between the eyes. I had to get out. Now.

I scrambled to find the key, hidden as always on the chimney mantle. Still blinded, somehow I managed to open the door, the handle slippery in my bloodied hands, the bolts struggling in vain against my efforts, I fled into the garden. Standing in the middle of the path, screaming, and screaming, and screaming, never, ever, ending, every night returning, piercing into my very being, the endless demons of the night.

The Asylum

My mind was muddled. That was all. I wasn't thinking right at all that day. I remember the rain, dripping from the trees all along the drive, the smell of damp leather in the car. My hands were tied. No - handcuffed. The metal cold on my wrists.

A nurse in long white apron, her hair unseen beneath a cap which covered her head. She did not look like an angel. She stood at the top of the steps and didn't reach out, or smile to greet me. Beside her, a man, severe in black uniform. It was he who took my arm and I was escorted in through revolving doors, doors to hell, I was soon to discover.

The officers who'd brought me to this place were keen to leave. It was a relief to have the metal cuffs removed, a relief which was short lived as I was bundled into a vicious-looking straitjacket before being led away down a long corridor to my future.

I don't want to remember what happened next and much of it is forgotten, or hidden safely away, deep inside some cavern in my mind. Still, sometimes pictures come back to the surface, unwelcome - a sound, a smell, a familiar voice or turn of phrase slap me in the face and remind me.

At first I was locked in a cell-like room, one of many off a long gallery where the worst of the women spent all of their days. They let me out only at set times, walked me to the bathroom and watched me whilst I used the toilet. The washed me - I had no dignity, didn't care if I stayed dirty, didn't care if they watched me, or if they laughed at me when they washed me. My daily routine was set to their clock. There was nothing left for me, you understand. I'd lost it all when the baby died. I never had a chance to say goodbye, never knew why she died, she just slipped away in the night.

The worst part of it was not saying goodbye, not being at her funeral. They all said it was my fault, that I'd been acting strangely and had smothered her in her cradle. I was lucky, they said - instead of going to the hangman, I was certified insane and brought here where I'd spend the rest of my days. I would be cared for, they said. Lucky me.

So, there I was, being cared for by asylum attendants and women dressed as nurses, angels of mercy. They had no mercy though. No-one had any sympathy for a woman who'd killed her only child. Why would they?

I had the best of all the modern treatments, of course. When my low mood seemed to be persisting they took me to the bath-house where I was forced to sit in a specially modified bath. I struggled as they pulled down the wooden lid which had a hole just big enough for my head to fit through. The lid was padlocked, water began to flow into the bath and continued flowing over me all the time I was in there. I was trapped, unable to free my arms which were inside the contraption. The female attendant who was watching me laughed even more as I struggled, my knees scraping against the inside of the rough wooden lid. The feeling of panic was overwhelming. It was for my own good. Afterwards, they dressed the cuts on my legs and bound my bleeding hands.

ECT was a double-edged sword. They told me it would cure me, but at what cost? And why would I want to be cured? That way would only lead to the gallows, surely? They said it wouldn't hurt. It did. They said I would feel better after each treatment. I may have done, but couldn't remember. What it really did for me was to wipe away all recent memory. I couldn't recall how well or how bad I'd been feeling. I even forgot were I was for a while, which was nice, and the names of those around me, sharing this asylum hell.

Then things started to change. A new broom was sweeping clean somewhere in the asylum. Some of the old attendants left, to be replaced by others who seemed more understanding of even the most violent of my fellow inmates. I was no longer locked in my room all day, now encouraged instead to mix with the other women in the gallery. I joined their weaving meanderings, pacing the vast space, sometimes sat at the windows, looking out at the courtyard and felt the sun on me from behind the safety of the glass. Occasionally, a group of us were taken out onto the grassy area below and were allowed to walk in the fresh air. Once a robin sang to me from the branch of a cherry tree. I felt an unfamiliar urge to laugh that day but I held it in as I knew they'd say it was madness laughter and anyway I had no right to be happy. So I pushed it away.

Life went on outside I suppose. I never knew because no-one ever came to visit. Not even you, the father of our daughter. I was told one day that I was no longer married. No one said anything but I could see in their eyes that they believed that I deserved to lose even you.

And so the world turns. I'm old now and have never known the growing up of children that I may have had. I've never worried about where they were when it got dark and they hadn't come home yet. The lines on my face are not the lines of a wise Grandmother. My life was over the day I was brought here to this asylum.

Inside Looking Out

The Sun's too bright through the window. There are no curtains. Even at night it's too bright when the moon is full. And it has been full, or nearly so, for the past few nights.

At least the sun is warm.

I look up and away from the window. I don't like the window. There's a crack there and I can hear the trees whispering to me through the gaps. But there's a crack in the wall too, in the plaster. It has the shape of a lightning bolt - it looks like it's making its way down the wall towards me like a step ladder from the ceiling. I wonder if there's a way out through the ceiling. But, no, that's just in my imagination. Sometimes I think that there's something hiding in the crack, spying on me. I tried to fill the crack to stop them being able to see me. The only thing I had to do this with was the mashed potato and mushy mince on my plate so I used that. I'd been made to eat in here because they said I was too disturbed to sit in the dining room. I wasn't allowed to have a knife and fork so they mashed up all my food. This was perfect for filling the crack in the wall but they caught me doing it and made me scrub it off with carbolic soap and water. And still the crack in the window is there, always whispering. I can't stop that. The trees are always watching me, watching and whispering through the window.

The orderlies leave me alone in the room but come along and look through the window of my door at me - They are watching me too, checking, checking on me all the time.

I look out of the window, squint in the sunlight. I can see the trees, so tall and majestic, like sentries watching over us all. Watching over those working in the fields. I wish I was sitting in the field of cabbages, working along the rows, crouching in the dusty dirt with the others. I can almost smell the cabbages from here - wish I had that dirt under my fingernails. There's a slight breeze ruffling the leaves with some kind of tantalising dance, scorning at me in its freedom.

I know what it's like, working in the field. That was my job before. Before the trees started whispering at me. They wouldn't let me be. I tried to tell them to stop, to leave me in peace. I liked the freedom of being outside in all weathers, loved the feel of rain on my face, running down my neck, cooling my desperate body. It was the only thing that kept me from going so far inside myself. And now, here I am, inside. All the time, inside.

I run my hands along the wall, feeling the zig-zag crack in the plaster. It's my only friend now. I can see inside the wall if I put my face right up against the plaster. Lick it. It tastes salty. I smile. I know who's living in there - little people with names and faces just like ours on the outside, inside. I mean, inside this place but outside of the wall itself. I'm not stupid - I know that it's not possible for any of us to get inside the wall - but there are people in there. I can hear them talking. Perhaps they come from the trees, whispering through the crack in the window, seeping through and creeping into the wall.

I want to go out but they'll never let me into the fields again, will they? I sat in an office wrapped up in a blanket - or was it a strait-jacket.? The Superintendent sat on the far side of the desk, not looking at me, but writing. He wanted me to explain but how could I? The words to tell what was happening to me, what had happened to me in the past, were buried deep down somewhere and anyway I knew he was one of them. One of the enemy, against me in everything I did. And he knew what I was thinking. I could tell because he was writing down everything and I wasn't even speaking yet. It's safer to stay quiet. Say nothing. Think nothing.

I can see out of the window the old man sitting by the gate, his easel facing towards the lane. He's painting the cabbages, rows and rows of cabbages. Why would he want to paint cabbages? And the trees which still move about in the breeze, he paints the trees too. I can just about make out from here the green on the canvas. I think he is lucky, free to do what he wants, even if it is only to paint cabbages and trees.

I liked the feel of the knife in my hand - the shiny, sharp knife, cutting through the cabbage stems at harvest time. I ran my finger along its blade sometimes, resisted the blade's edge, enjoying the cold feel of steel against my skin. I could still be there now if only the trees hadn't spoken to me, told me to cut myself. And I did cut myself - my left ear, just like a cabbage - I cut it off. It didn't hurt. The orderly looking after us didn't notice at first - he was sitting on the bench at the edge of the field, smoking and day-dreaming. Then he must have heard the screaming - I think it was me screaming, so he came across to look. I can't remember any more about that day.

The superintendent said it was me. I couldn't be trusted with knives any more. Not since I'd cut off my ear and stabbed the orderly.

I look at the door. It's always locked. There's a shadow across the window. It must be time for them to come and get me. They're coming to take me to the treatment room. Well, they call it treatment but they don't like me - they say I'm evil, but I'm not.

Ella's Tale

My name's Ella - a name which may be familiar to many of you. I have to make it quite clear though, I DO NOT spend any time in the kitchen and have never messed about with anything to do with the fireplace!

I recognised his face on a poster advertising a three night festival, designed, apparently, to attract young women who if they were lucky, might stand a chance of being chosen by Princey as 'the one'. How sexist is that? How dare he imagine that there could be any women alive today who'd be satisfied with just being some spoilt man's wife. Though maybe I was wrong on that point. If you knew what he'd done to my sister you wouldn't go there.

To prepare myself for the festival, I went shopping. I had to have the outfit to make sure that the Prince didn't recognise me and his eyes were on no-one else but me. And of course, there had to be those Killer Heels. There's that little shop in the precinct - Godmother's. I knew I'd find the right kind of magic there.

The evening arrived. I donned my carefully chosen gown and looked at myself in the mirror. My sister's image smiled back at me in approval. I held her eyes for a long moment before she disappeared and slipped on my shoes as the limo arrived to whisk me to the opening gala night.

When we pulled up outside the Palace Ballroom I could see the Prince standing at the top of the flight of stairs. Crowds of noisy, cheering people lined the red carpet which led up to where he stood. But it was when my driver opened the door to the limo and I began to step out that a hush fell on the crowd. The first thing to be seen was a red stiletto-heeled shoe, followed by my slender stockinged leg.

The Prince was hooked in that moment. No longer content to wait at the top of the flight, he ran swiftly down the staircase and took my hand to brush it with his lips, lips which were cold, I have to say. The spectators were in awe, wondering, no doubt, as to who this mysterious woman could be, all so jealous of the Prince's attention to me as we swept up to the entrance, my black lace gown clinging to every curve, revealing the black basque I wore underneath. The only splash of colour, my red lips, red nails and of course, the killer red stilettos.

The Prince would not let me out of his sight. We danced every dance. At midnight, he took me outside into the garden. He was all over me.

"You've got to be mine," he purred into my ear.

He thinks he's a bloody cat! But I smiled.

He put his hand on my knee, sliding it unceremoniously up my thigh towards the top of my stockinged leg. "Sorry, Princey," I said. "Time for me to fly away."

I was out of his arms and flitting through the garden towards the gate before he could take a breath. My limo was waiting, as pre-arranged, just beyond the gate, and I was in it and away in the twinkling of an eye. I laughed all the way home. And no, it did not turn into a pumpkin on the way.

The following day, waiting for the limo to arrive, I again stood before the mirror. My sister appeared beside me, as before, and smiled. "Take care," she whispered. "Remember to take care."

"I will," I said.

She blew me a kiss before her image faded.

I lounged in the back of the limo as we drove through the streets, excited at the thought of seeing the Prince again and there he was, waiting at the top of the staircase as before. He flew down the steps to the car. This time he didn't wait for the driver to open the door but did so himself, bowing to me as he reached for my hand to kiss.

His lips were still cold.

"You look even more beautiful, if that's possible," he whispered. He helped me from the car, his arm around me as we took the steps, slowly and regally, my black lace dress again revealing my under-garments, once more the only colour the red of my lips, my painted nails and the killer red stiletto heeled shoes.

We danced for just an hour before he made his move.

"I need to be alone with you." He led me to a room at the end of a corridor. "Why did you leave me so suddenly last night? I wanted you so much."

"I wanted you, too," I smiled. "But, too much, too soon. You wouldn't have respected me in the morning."

He laughed. "You came back, that's all that matters. I expect you'd like a glass of champagne."

I looked around the room. There was a table laid with sumptuous food. "Come and sit here." He led me to the table and began to feed me morsels of food from the various dishes. To feed me! I don't know how I contained myself but I did. I sat there and simpered at him. Me, simpering! I had him. I let him put things into my mouth that I never would normally even look at - gorgonzola, spicy kebabs, chocolate-coated bacon. He pushed a ripe strawberry between my lips, the sticky juice ran down my chin, my neck and into my cleavage. His lips were on my breasts, his tongue licking the sweetness from my skin.

"You're driving me mad," he groaned.

I pushed him away. "Too soon, too soon." And I was on my feet and moving towards the door.

The door was locked. "You can't go yet," he said. "I can't let you run off like you did last night."

"Who do you think I am?" I asked. "Do you have no respect for me?"

He was so charming. "I think you're leading me on," he leered. "You know you want me. Otherwise why did you come?"

I smiled back at him. "You're right," I said. "I did made the decision to come back. I enjoyed the dance. Let me go now and I promise I'll be here again tomorrow evening and I'll fulfill your wildest desires."

I could almost hear his thoughts for a moment. The clock striking midnight completed the spell as he unlocked the door and let me go. Foolish man!

On the final evening, I was ready for him. As I donned the killer red stilettos I felt wonderful, full of power.

My sister was waiting for me as I stood in front of the mirror.

"Now is the time," I said. "Now he will pay for what he did to you."

The Prince was waiting at the foot of the staircase. The car had barely come to a halt when he flung open the door. He gasped when he saw me. "You look amazing," he said as he helped me out.

He held himself back whilst we danced, as though distracted. I wondered what was going through his mind. It wasn't long before I found out. After only one dance, he led me up a further flight of stairs into a room in a quiet corridor.

He took me in his arms. "I can't wait any longer." With his cold lips he kissed me, his hands on my neck, my shoulders and on my breasts.

"Wait," I said. "It's too soon, too soon."

"Don't tease me. You promised." He was backing me across the room towards a wide, silk-covered bed. "You know you want me."

"Not like this," I protested but he'd already pushed me down and held me there. "I can't let you go this time." His hands pulled at my clothes.

"Wait!" I cried. "Let me do it myself."

He hesitated for only a moment. I looked into his black eyes I and knew that I had won. He released his grip. I rolled off the bed and stood up.

"Stay there," I smiled down at him as I took from my bag the cords that I'd been longing to use. "I want to make this special for both of us."

I tied him to the bed posts, his eyes hungry for me. "So handsome," I said. "Every woman's dream, aren't you? Are you ready for me?"

His lips were wet in anticipation. My eyes swept over his body. He was indeed, ready. I was ready too. As I peeled off the black lace dress there was a flicker of recognition in his eyes, a flash of fear. I laughed as I slipped off one of my killer red stilettos and before he knew what was happening I'd thrust the heel into his heart and we were as one, the pulsing heat of his life's force spilling into mine.

He groaned.

"Too soon," I whispered "Just like my sister did, I told you it was too soon.'"

I smiled as I dressed and I left, my only regret was having to leave behind one of my killer red stilettos.

Dear John

He's living in this street. It's dark now but I know that shop on the corner. It's the same one I hid inside the day he came to town. A wide and busy thoroughfare with room for carriages to pass. I had watched as he stepped from the steamer at Clarence Pier - watched and followed him as he walked to this street, carrying his bag like he owned the space that he walked on.

That is the house. That one there. I know it's just like any other building in this street. It's squashed in between the Bush Hotel and the Church, but this one is different, special, because he is in there. The front door is imposing, with fan-light windows above. There's a flickering light in the hall. They can't have been converted from gas yet. Good. That'll make it all the more easy for me.

Let me make it clear at this point. I didn't want this to happen. I wouldn't have even considered this if they had taken notice of me when I went to them for help. All the way to Baker Street I went, on the train - nasty, dirty, smelly things but a quick way to get to London and back in a day. That way I could do it without anyone noticing that I was missing. They thought I was visiting my Mama. Little did they ever imagine that I was seeking a way to slay all the demons from my past. It was what I needed to do.

It was easy to convince them that I was cured of all my bad habits, as they called them. Easy, because in there there is little chance to act immorally - except of course with that attendant who used to come into my room at night and make me do it. He said that was what I wanted.

After the child was born, so long, long ago, they took me to that place, for my own good. They said I was ill, mad, immoral. I don't know what happened to the child.

He came to me time after time. I told no-one. He said I enticed him, whatever that means. I used to wish he was dead, that he would fall under a carriage or into the canal.

During the days in there we never saw a man except when the Superintendent visited the ward, which was rarely. Mostly we were taken to his office. Only women cared for us, if you could call it care. But at night the male attendant would visit me. He shouldn't have been there. Once I saw money change hands when the woman in charge let him into my room. I heard the key turning in the lock after he came in and we were alone.

I don't recall how long it went on for but one night there was a new woman in charge and that's when the visits stopped.

After a time I was moved to a dormitory and eventually they started letting me out - with a nurse at first - to walk in the lanes or to visit my Mama. For the past few months I've been allowed out by myself. It was on one of these occasions that I found the bundle of letters in Mama's bureau, letters which revealed the truth behind it all. I had never told them who the father was but it appeared that Mama knew all along. How could I have told when it was my cousin, John. Not only my cousin, but a respected member of the community - a Doctor, who had lodged in our home whilst he worked for a while in Portsmouth. The letters were from him and clearly had his address on them. Mama was surprised when I told her that I'd found the letters and she was even more surprised when she tripped on a loose carpet and fell down the stairs.

They let me go to the funeral. I looked out for John but he wasn't there. Now I go to visit Mama in the cemetery instead.

I never thought that I would see him again - he lived in London now and was famous. I saw his name in the paper - they let us read them sometimes, said it was good for us to keep in touch with the World. I was shocked when I read what he'd been up to - assisting that Sherlock Holmes in those murder cases. A respected upholder of the law now, when all I could think about was what he had done to me all that time ago. He had just walked away with not a thought for me. The headline in the paper mentioned Holmes of Baker Street. Well, it was easy enough to make my way to the City and once on the street a passer-by pointed me to the right house.

John was not happy to see me, made out that I was a lunatic. Well, maybe I am. Mr. Holmes was there too but he was distracted by something in another room and did not seem interested in me. I remember him muttering to John that he should take better care of his mad relatives before he left

79

the room. As I was ushered back down the stairs by the housekeeper, I could hear the strains of a violin. How I despise that sound.

Perhaps something turned in my mind that day, perhaps I always was a bit insane. If John had only acknowledged my pain and what had happened between us, I might have forgiven him and then I'd not be here tonight.

I've come prepared. I have got everything here in my bag - paper, petrol, an old rag to soak and matches. I will push the paper through the letter box, then the lighted petrol-soaked rag. When it lands on the doormat they won't know what's hit them. It will be too late, and it will serve them right, both of them.

Nightmare

Carol stood up, doing up the buttons on her coat, and got off the bus at her usual stop. She walked hastily along the street, without a glance to either side, her stiletto heels tap-tapping on the shiny paving slabs. All around her was dark and glistening, as though the city had been cleaned especially for this moment.

She turned the corner away from the High Street, and bent her head against the weather, the rain like needles piercing her skin. Her mind was full of what was to come. "Oh, God," she whispered to herself, "Let it be easy. Please let it work."

Maybe because she was so pre-occupied, she missed the warning signs, didn't see the man in the doorway, his face turned away from the road. Whatever the reason, she was not on form that night. Suddenly a face loomed into hers. It was too late to do anything other than make a stand.

"What the hell do you think you're doing?" Her voice was high and squeaky, hardly the voice of authority.

"Yer bag. Gimme yer bag." His breath was fetid, and sweet, like fermenting apples in a compost heap.

"Not my bag. No, please. I'll give you the money. My purse." She groped in her bag, trying to find her purse, panicking.

"Gimme yer fuckin' bag. Slag!" He spat in her face.

Carol held tightly on to her bag, a feeling of anger rising to the surface. Realising that he seemed to have no weapon, and was, in fact, quite a skinny guy, she decided to call his bluff. After all, what did she have to lose?

"How dare you! Go away! Help! Help!" She cried.

A flash of metal glinted in the gloom of the dimly-lit street. "You stupid bitch," he growled.

Carol felt the knife slash across her face. A short, sharp, shocking pain, a feeling of disbelief in her stomach. She heard his footsteps running away, splashing in the puddles of the uneven footpath, as the paving stones slid up to slap her in the face. She remembered the cold underneath her, and thinking, "my new coat, it'll get wet if I lie here." Then, sweet darkness.

"She's coming round," a voice in the distance seemed to be shouting across a void.

"Carol. Hello, Carol, are you alright?" The voice was getting closer. She felt the pressure of a hand on her shoulder, gently shaking her awake. But Carol didn't want to wake up. She had a feeling that whatever had happened, it could only get worse. Bright lights were trying to force their way into her eyelids.

"Is she conscious? We need to speak to her." A different voice, harsh and urgent.

"Would you please wait outside." The first voice, taking control of the situation.

"I have authority to speak to her as soon as she wakes up."

"Well, when she wakes up, I will let you know. Now, please wait outside."

Carol held her breath until she heard the door swing shut. She was afraid to open her eyes to the reality of this situation. If only she could stay unconscious for a little longer. She remembered that trick she used to do when she was a kid. You could open your eyes just a fraction, and still look as though you were asleep. It had fooled her parents.

She lay still, listening, heard the other person in the room move away from her bedside. She decided to risk opening her eyes, and as she did so the light almost blinded her, even through the tiny gap between her eyelashes. She turned her head slightly, but even that small movement was too much. Too much for the pain in her head, and too much for the nurse not to have noticed.

She was at Carol's bedside within one blink. "Hello, Carol. Now don't try to move at all. You've had a nasty shock, your hands are cut and you've had a bump on the head. You must try to rest. You are in hospital."

"My bag; where's my bag?" Carol tried to keep her voice to a whisper, but it sounded too loud, like someone shouting in her head.

"All your things are in a black bin liner beside your bed. Do you want me to see if your bag is there?"

"Please..."

The door swung open again and before the nurse could stop him, a stockily built figure had entered.

"I told you that you should wait outside. This is a

hospital, and I am the nurse in charge here. Now will you please leave."

"Look. I really need to speak to Mrs. Parker. Urgently! Mrs. Parker, DC Barnes." He flashed a badge near to Carol's face. She shuddered.

The nurse looked at Carol questioningly. "O.K., I'll be alright," she said in reply.

"Well, just a few minutes, then. And then you must leave her to rest."

She stood by the door, like a sentry guarding a precious jewel, glaring at the man.

"Now, Mrs. Parker, I need you to tell me what happened last night. How did you get in this state?"

"I don't know. Some man in the shadows. Didn't see his face."

"A man in the shadows? Let's start from the beginning."

"I got off the bus, and was walking up the High Street. I turned the corner, along The Avenue, and he was there, I think, in some doorway. He had a hoodie on. I couldn't see him. My mind was on other things."

"Did he speak to you?"

"I don't think so. Yes, he said 'Give me your bag.'"

"And did you?"

"No. I thought he was bluffing. He had no weapon, I thought."

"So what did you do?"

"I called for help. Told him to go away," Carol

laughed nervously. "How stupid was that, eh?"

"Then what happened?"

"I can't remember. I think he cut my face." Carol's left hand flew to her face, where she'd felt the sharp blade slashing her.

"There's no cut on your face now, Mrs. Parker."

"There must be." Panic was setting in, as Carol's hand scanned both her cheeks. There was nothing, her skin as smooth as it ever had been.

The nurse moved away from the door. "That's enough now, DC Barnes."

"Just a few more questions."

"I said, enough. You will leave, now!"

"O.K., I'm going. But I will be back. This is a murder investigation. I will need to speak to you again, Mrs. Parker, and a police officer will be on duty outside this room at all times." He turned and left the room. She could see him through the glass observation window, talking to a uniformed police woman.

Carol's head was awash with questions. "Murder investigation? Who's murder?" She didn't realise that she had spoken out loud.

The nurse was by her side once more. "They found his body in a doorway, I think."

"What do you mean?"

"He was dead."

"Who? I heard him running away." Carol's mind was spinning, trying to remember. "My bag - please can you find my bag?" She watched desperately as the nurse rummaged in the bin liner, and felt relief wash over her as her bag was revealed, intact, just as she'd last seen it.

"There you are." The nurse placed the bag on the bed, carefully avoiding the bandages on Carol's right hand. Carol relaxed into the pillows, clutching her bag to her chest as she drifted off to sleep.

Her oblivion was short-lived. Within minutes the doubts in her dreamlike state niggled her awake again. Her bag was still there, held tightly in her hand. She brought it closer to her face and clumsily opened it with her good hand. A quick peak inside, just to put her mind at rest, but nothing prepared her for the horror that was waiting there. The bag dropped from her hand. Carol heard something clatter on the polished floor. She tried to raise up from her pillows to reach over the side of the bed, but there was no strength left in her. Then she realised that the nurse was beside her again, but this time there was fear in her eyes.

"Please..." Carol began, but the nurse had already pressed the call button. The door opened with urgency and another nurse appeared at the door.

"You'd better get that police woman in here," she indicated the object under the bed. "Don't touch it. Just get the officer in here." She looked at Carol apologetically. "I am sorry, but I have a duty if I think you are a risk to yourself or others."

"How pompous that sounds," Carol thought. "I really don't know how that got in my bag," she said. "Please, help me."

Too late. The police woman was already in the room. Taking a plastic bag from her pocket, and donning a pair of gloves, she carefully picked up the bloody knife and placed it in the bag.

"It was in her handbag," the nurse said, glancing apologetically at Carol.

"I don't know how it got in there. I've never seen it before," stammered Carol. "You have to believe me."

"Now, just calm down, Mrs. Parker. I'm going to call the DC back. He'll want to have another chat with you."

Carol's mind was racing. How had it come to this? The evening had started exactly as she'd planned. Her night out with Alison as usual. Then it had all gone wrong after she'd got off the bus. The knife in her bag; the same knife that the man had in the street. Attacking her was not part of the deal, and she could have sworn that he slashed her face, before running away, but now he was dead, instead of....?

"Nurse, I need to see Tom, my husband. He'll be worrying about me."

"Of course. I'll get the phone trolley."

"Don't you worry about your husband, Mrs. Parker," the police woman interjected. "An officer will have been to your house. We've got all your details from your wallet. It was in your coat pocket." She looked at the nurse. "Don't know how we missed your bag, though. Should have checked the contents as soon as you came in. Wasting police time," she grumbled.

Carol was shaking inside, wondering what the police would find when they got to the house. Before she could think the situation through any further, the door opened again.

"Hello, Carol." It was Tom, followed closely by DC Barnes.

Carol closed her eyes in despair.

Asylum Night

Late for night shift again, I hurried along Locksway Road. I was not looking forward to another long night at St. James and would have loved to have been snuggled up in front of the t.v. for a mindless evening of soaps.

I stood at the foot of the tree-lined avenue. The night was bright - as bright as any day. I stared at the sky; the moon was full. I pulled my jacket closer to me, shivering, and found myself being drawn towards the looming ancient building, its clock tower's face grinning menacingly at me as I approached.

The trees which overhung the avenue were still - no wind, not even the slightest breeze. Everything seemed unreal, no night-owls, no rustling of creatures in the undergrowth. Just me, the night and the gothic windows of the house at the end of the drive. I was about halfway along when I noticed a figure in one of the windows staring out at me. It was a woman dressed in the uniform of a nurse from the last century. A long dark dress covered in a white apron, her sleeves were cuffed at the wrists and her hair was caught up in a triangular white head-dress, like the caps nurses wore in the time of the First World War. As I moved a little closer I waved but she didn't seem to see me.

I reached the revolving doors and pushed my way through. I was curious to meet this figure I'd seen but which room was she in? I looked about me at the wood-panelled walls, at the stern faces of past medical superintendents in ornately framed portraits, proudly displaying outrageous whiskers. Eyes appeared to follow me as I walked about the room which was familiar but strange in some way. I remembered passing through this room so many times on my way to take up my duties but those memories were slipping away somehow.

The wooden-framed glass doors swung open easily as I passed through to the bottom of a sweeping staircase. I trembled a little as I took the stairs one by one, trying hard not to let their creaks echo in the hallway. I looked up at the domed skylight high above me and in the light of the moon I swear I saw a figure again, leaning over the bannister, silhouetted, staring down at me. I blinked and looked again - she was gone. I wondered if I'd imagined it, shook away the fear and continued to climb up towards my fate.

Soon reaching the first floor, the heavy-looking doors on the landing were all tightly closed. I hesitated to try any of them, never having been in this part of the building before - it had always seemed to be out of bounds. In fact, I wondered what had made me even venture onto the staircase at all. I waited and listened but all was silent - uncannily so. 'Pull yourself together woman,' I scolded myself, trying not to think about the tales of past residents of this place and the early treatments for the mentally ill. I was about to take to the stairs again, still curious to find the mysterious woman I'd seen, when I heard a faint scratching sound coming from behind the double doors set in the centre of the landing.

I stood before them for what seemed like a million heartbeats, the scratching sound persistently leading me on. I gripped the door knob, felt the cold metal in my hand for a moment, hesitated and stepped backwards, losing my nerve. As I was about to return to the staircase, a movement caught my eye. The door knob was turning by itself. 'Someone must be on the other side of the door.' I felt myself sway slightly in fear with the knowledge that I was about to come face to face with - what? Or who?

Before I could bring myself to turn and run the door swung open to reveal a sight that I found completely confusing. A man dressed in the costume of an Edwardian gentleman stood in front of me.

'Well, Mrs. Bennett,' he smiled. 'What are you doing, wandering about on the stairs, my dear?' he reached his hand out to me and gripped my wrist. I looked down at his hand and tried to pull myself away but he was too strong. He dragged me into the room.

'Please, let me go,' I protested. 'What the hell is going on? Who are you?'

At that moment, the doors behind me closed with a bang. I turned my head to find another figure had entered the room. This time it was a woman, the same woman I'd seen at the window and later on the stairs. Her long apron was crisply white, as was the starched collar at her neck and the cuffs at her wrists. Her hair was hidden by the triangular headdress of her uniform. Her eyes bored into me as she crossed the room. I struggled again, laughing nervously. 'Please let me go,' I begged. I assumed that I'd wandered in on some kind of party or film set but I had to get to work. 'I'm due on duty in five minutes and I'll be late.'

The nurse looked at me with pity in her eyes, then past me at the man. 'You were right Doctor,' she said. 'Mrs. Bennett is completely deluded. We will have to start the treatment again, and the sooner the better.'

'What do you mean? Doctor?' I was panicking now. 'Stop this messing about, please.' Realising he looked just like one of the men in the paintings downstairs, I hesitated, then went on. 'Come on, this is silly. Some sort of game.' My mind was racing. I was sure that they must be making some sort of film about the old asylum and I'd walked in on their rehearsals. But where were the cameras? I assumed that they hadn't arrived yet. Actually I don't know what I assumed. I couldn't seem to think straight at all any more.

'Just give me a moment, nurse.' The man was speaking over my head. He turned to me. 'Now, Mrs. Bennett, we have given you a lot of time with the new psycho-analytical treatment and yet you still seem no better than when you first arrived here two years ago.'

'Two years!' I screamed. 'What on earth are you going on about? I work here. I've worked here for two years. I'm on my way to the ward for night duty. I have a family at home waiting for me.'

'It's alright Mrs. Bennett.' The nurse was speaking now, her voice soft and calming. 'You're safe now, back at the asylum. We'll take good care of you.'

The doctor smiled as he spoke but what he said next sent a bolt of cold fear through me.

'I'm afraid we will have to start the hydrotherapy treatment again, nurse. And I think some time in the padded cell in a straight-jacket, for her own good, you understand, just to calm her down.'

Of course I struggled. I screamed and kicked, thinking of my husband and children waiting at home in the morning. They would be wondering where I was and why I hadn't come home from work. The more I fought, the worse it got. At first I thought I could get away and I did break free from their grasp but even before I reached the doors they flew open and there stood four more nurses, all dressed in the same old fashioned uniforms. One of them held a straight-jacket, just like the one in the museum in town. I still believed they were playing some kind of misguided and evil trick on me but here I am in this padded cell, trussed up with the promise of being forced into a bath of running water as soon as the day staff come on duty.

After Show Party

The auditorium was quiet now, the after show party had fizzled out, the last few stragglers long gone home and Amy was left alone. She sat on the edge of the stage and looked up towards the back of the theatre, red plush seats like rows of soldiers standing to attention, gazing blankly back at her.

Playing Lady Macbeth had been amazing - demanding the depths of feelings - anger, madness, passion - and she'd never felt so close to a leading man before. Tom's Macbeth was stunning and between them they'd caused a sensation. Still elated from the final applause and the congratulations from other cast members, Amy could also sense the grief which seeps in gradually at the end of a run. She knew what to expect. Within three days a black despair would descend and she'd be trapped, doubting herself, unable to see any future.

The voices of the cast echoed to her, 'Here's to the next one!' 'Will miss you darling!' 'We must keep in touch!' 'You were marvellous!' Their voices faded as Amy brought herself to her feet.

Wondering where Tom was, she walked into the wings. As she passed the small props table she noticed that it hadn't been cleared properly. The dagger was there in its place, as if set for the next show. 'Well there won't be any more of those,' she thought as she took up the blade, planning to leave it with the night-watchman on her way out. Then as she turned away towards the stage door she saw them. Tom and the Third Witch. And they were kissing. More than kissing - his hands were all over her and she was obviously enjoying it. Amy was shocked and let out a short gasp. The couple stopped and Tom looked across at Amy.

It was the way he smiled at her that made her do it - a smug, winning kind of smile - but his eyes were hard and cold.

The dagger slid in so easily. It was as if it were one of those toy daggers that retracted into its handle whilst looking as though it were sinking into flesh. Tom stopped smiling after the fifth plunge. As he sank to the wooden floor, Amy watched the river of blood running across the raked stage and wondered fleetingly where the Third Witch had gone. Then she turned to the auditorium and took a bow. The red plush soldiers gazed blankly back at her as she sat on the edge of the stage to wait.

A String of Pearls

My name is Pearl. I was named after my Grandmother who was a nursing auxiliary during the war in the 1940s. She was a beautiful woman. I've got a photograph of her in uniform, handed down to me with this old necklace. The pearls don't look much now - I don't suppose they're real and the clasp is tarnished. Still, they mean a lot to me. When I hold them in my hands it's almost like I'm looking down a tunnel into the past, into the history of my family.

I went back to the house in town where she'd lived once, long after she and Granddad were gone. It still felt like she'd only just left the room, popped out for a packet of tea or something. Of course, it was all in my imagination - she didn't even live there anymore and hadn't for years.

After the war, my Grandmother had married my wonderful Granddad; he was a sailor during the war and worked in the docks afterwards. They only had one child, my Mother, who was born quite soon after they got married. No-one in the family told me but I worked it out when I was very young that Gran must have been pregnant on their wedding day. Shocking, eh?

I never saw Gran wearing the pearls and didn't even know about them until after she died. I was only six years old but can still see her face, smiling at me from her bed just a few days before she went. She left me a box of things and the pearls were tucked inside an old brown envelope at the bottom of the box. Mum said she'd never seen them before. She thought that they couldn't have been worth anything much. Gran and Granddad went through tough times after the war and had to sell everything that was of any value. The necklace would have been the first thing to go, she'd thought.

I sometimes take them out and just hold them in my hands - the smooth pearls feel warm to my touch. Then today I had this urge to go down to Old Portsmouth. I dropped the necklace into my pocket and walked through the town. I sat on the wall by the Square Tower and looked at the sea. I could sense the pearls in my pocket, almost calling me to take them out and breathe in the fresh brine. The tide was high, the waves smashed against the shingle, loud and dangerous, splashing spray up towards my feet. I held the pearls to my cheek and could feel them tingling against my skin.

So immersed as I was in the power of the elements and this link with my Grandmother in my hand, I hadn't noticed that I was no longer alone. It was only when I felt the touch of a hand on my shoulder that I jumped with a start. I stood and turned to see a man was standing beside me. A stranger, but somehow familiar. He was dressed quite oddly, I thought later, although at the time I hardly noticed what he was wearing. It was his face, his eyes, that struck me at that time. He was smiling at me.

"My Pearl," he said. "You waited. I knew you would."

I wondered how he knew my name. I wondered what he meant when he said that I had waited for him. I had never seen him before. And yet....

He took the pearls from my hand. "Allow me. Turn around." I turned as he gently placed the pearls around my neck. He spun me around to face him once more. "There, perfect." He took my hand and lifted it to his lips. I was powerless to do anything other than stand there but his lips were cold and it felt wrong somehow, to be kissed like that by a stranger. I pulled away and looked at him.

"Who are you?" I asked.

He frowned. "You don't know me? But of course you do. I promised I would come back for you, remember? I know I've been away for a long time, but you said you would wait for me. I gave you the pearls - you know I gave you the pearls - instead of an engagement ring. The pearls were my Mother's. I promised I would marry you and now I'm back."

"No, these pearls were given to me by my Grandmother," I started to explain, but he didn't seem to be listening. He just gazed out to sea and carried on talking.

"I got your letter about the child. I know it must have been hard for you, being on your own, but I promised to marry you and now I'm here. How long is it now before the child is due?"

I stared at him, horrified. "The child?"

"Our child," he said. "I've been longing to see you for so long. Now we can be a family at last."

"But all that happened a long time ago," I said, trying to find the right way to tell him, not being quite sure myself what was happening. This was probably a joke, someone who knew a bit about my family, trying to make a fool out of me. But why? I decided to put a stop to this straight away. "My Grandmother - she married someone else. It's not me, it was my Grandmother you gave these pearls to - you, or someone else - over fifty years ago."

It was then that the pearls fell from my neck. The string, being old and weak, broke and the pearls tumbled to the ground, bouncing off the wall onto the beach below. I cried out and scrabbled around, trying to save them from being lost amongst the shingle. I think I managed to find most of them, and placed them safely inside my coat pocket.

By the time I'd stood up and looked about me the man had gone. It had started to rain and there was nobody about. I shivered, turned up my coat collar and walked home, the pearls still warm in my pocket.

A Slice of Toast

There I am, one day, just walking back from dropping my car off at the workshop, feeling real good about myself and determined to enjoy the morning sun. I'm thinking about losing weight and wondering how long it'll take to get home. The walk should take about an hour, I figure, when I come across this lollipop lady, standing by the roadside. She's all trussed up in layers of knitted garments topped by a bright yellow waistcoat, looking out from under her grimy peaked cap and I'm thinking that there is something vaguely familiar in the way she is leaning on her lollipop.

Well, she's just standing there, you know, waiting for the last kids to come along. I look at my watch and I'm thinking, "well, most kids should be at school by now." The woman looks at me kinda strange and I try not to look her in the eye. So my eyes are wandering this way and that, anything other than in her direction.

Then I notice a slice of toast lying in the gutter. A plain, white slice, with no butter, and I get to thinking about it and wondering how it got there. Was it dropped by the woman, or by some kid in its hurry to cross the road? Maybe it was thrown from the open window of a passing truck, or maybe something else happened. Now, my natural curiosity has been known to be my downfall, but sometimes I just can't help myself from getting involved in interesting situations.

I don't know how long these thoughts are passing through my brain, maybe a split second, but I start to notice that the woman is looking at me like she knows more than she wants to let on. I decide to hang about a while to see what develops. It's getting a bit uncomfortable here though, so I just stroll on down the street and turn the corner.

There's this bench just around the corner and it's tucked away, real convenient like, out of sight of the lollipop lady, and I sense that she'll be passing the end of the street soon, so I decide to wait, and sure enough, there she goes, right on cue, back to her little home in some other side-street. I don't want to let her out of my sight, so I scurry off after her, taking care of course to keep a discrete distance, just in case she twigs that she's being followed, you understand.

Now, the road goes this way and that, and after some time, and many turnings, she dips out of sight for a while. One minute she's there, and the next she's not. I'm not too worried about this though because it's one of those streets where the houses have front gardens with long paths that go right up to the front door, and there's no way she could get inside one of these places without me seeing her, so I figure I'd have plenty of time to get a good view of whatever she's up to.

So, there I am, hanging about on the street corner, wondering what to do next, and thinking that maybe it's time to move on and forget all about the whole idea, when I realise that she's standing right there behind me. I kinda sense her before I see her. I'm standing there, minding someone else's business and then I get this creepy feeling down the back of my neck. Next thing I know, I turn around, and there she is, just standing there, staring down at me. I say staring down, being as she's a lot taller than me. Not that I'm short, you understand. Just that she is much taller. She looks me in the eye and a slow smile creeps over her face, the eyes twinkling at me. Yes, you heard right, they were twinkling, you know, like when you're really happy to see someone.

Well, she grabs my shoulders and then she's got her arms right around me, and I'm in the vice-like grip of her embrace. I don't know what to make of all this, but I get swept up in it and find myself being marched off down the street in mid-hug with this lady who's gushing all over me to come in for a cup of coffee.

Now, I'm very particular about my coffee, and I just can't drink that stuff that comes in granules out of screw-top jars, but I can't get away without causing offence, so I decide to go along with it, and by the time we get to her house, I feel like we're old pals. Not like pals you see every day, or even every week, you know. No, I mean like, say, an old school pal that you haven't seen for years, someone you've been out of touch with for a reason you can't quite remember.

Anyway, we reach the front door and it's like stepping into the fifties, if you know what I mean. You may not remember that far back, of course, but then you may have seen it in the movies. Well, I tell you, as soon as I step onto that grey linoleum floor, there I am, back in my childhood, every memory intact, even down to the faint smell of yesterday's boiled fish.

I soon snap out of it as she's disappearing into the back of the house, turning once to beckon me on with a definite air of impatience. That was when I notice her long painted fingernails. Well, you don't expect lollipop ladies to be going about with long painted fingernails do you?

So, I find myself meandering towards the kitchen door wondering at the same time exactly what I'm getting myself into. It's as I pass the half-opened door under the stairs that I start to feel uneasy. I can't quite put my finger on what's going on but swear that I can smell something else behind the fish - something more appealing - chocolate perhaps. The kitchen's a cosy little room and I'm sitting at the table waiting while she puts the coffee on. It's a real coffee maker, no jar of instant in sight. I can tell you, I'm quite relieved at this. As I've said before, instant coffee does nothing for me.

The next thing I know is that she's offering me breakfast with my coffee. Now, as I have previously indicated, I'm thinking seriously about losing weight and the thought of eating another breakfast is pretty unwelcome at that moment. I'm just about to decline the offer, when she turns around, and there she is, holding out to me a plate of toast.

I take one look at her, then another at the toast, and start putting two and two together in my mind and making five. I had seen that slice of toast somewhere before, or one very much like it. Now, you might say I have a vivid imagination, but I do not want to go down the same route as whoever the owner of the said slice may have been tempted.

That's when I decide to humour her, hoping that I'll be able to blag my way out of what could be a sticky situation. So I find myself smiling back at her as sweetly as I can, and ask her if she has any marmalade. Of course, she would have marmalade, and home-made at that, so I'm thinking that maybe I'm in for a treat.

It's not long before the coffee pot is bubbling, the aroma disguising the stale smell of fish which stubbornly wraps itself around the curtains at the grimy kitchen window, and I'm thinking to myself thoughts of what else it might be disguising.

As she places the toast in front of me and hands me the jar or marmalade, this is when I decide that it's time to make myself scarce. So I'm sitting there thinking about how I can slip away without her getting upset. She looks the type of woman that you just don't get on the wrong side of, you know, but I just have the feeling that I have to get out of there. Something was just telling me it was time to split.

So, there I am, listening to my heart beating so loud that I am sure she can hear the blood pumping through my veins. Then I get my chance. There's a tapping at the kitchen window, and as she goes over to look out, that's when I make a break for it. Before I can re-assess what I am doing, well, I'm legging it down the garden path, out of the gate, and off down the street as fast as I can.

As I pass the spot where the lollipop lady stands to help the kids across the road, I toss away the slice of toast that somehow was still in my hand as I made my escape. It skims across the path and lands face-down in the gutter, right next to the very same slice I had seen less than an hour before.

The Reunion

The train pulled in and I waited. Just inside the cafe, watching from the window, I could see the passengers bustling through the gates from the platform. I wanted to run away but it was too late. There was nowhere to run without being seen. Looking back, I don't know why I felt like that. Seeing you again was what I'd longed for wasn't it?

It was three years since you'd been gone. We stood on that platform then, on the day you left. I held onto your jacket lapels, the wool harsh against my fingers. I can still smell your cologne and remember the smoothness of your newly shaved cheek as I held my face next to yours, reluctant to let you see that the sparkle in my eyes was caused by tears, not joy.

I put my arms around you as you held me close. We savoured every last second that we were together, in the knowledge that it could be a long time before we would meet again. I clung onto every part of you, stored you in my memory. Each time I have longed for you, I have drunk from the well of happy thoughts that I'd stored away in those last moments that we were together.

And now you were coming home. I was afraid that it would not be the same - that the years apart would have changed you as I am sure that they had changed me. Three years isn't very long when you are together, but three years apart is an age when so many things have been experienced by both of us, things that the other would never know about, not fully. Words on sheets of paper can never share the truth of how life can effect you. You would not understand what I had been through just as I could not understand the things that you have had to do.

There have been times when I lost heart and looked to others for comfort. Now I feel ashamed that I had to do that although at the time it seemed the only way that I could get through the loneliness. And I am sure that you have had times, too, when you sought solace elsewhere. I won't be jealous but I hope that you don't think you have to share anything with me that may have happened. I don't want to know. Just tell me you still love me and have longed for this moment as much as I have. That is all I ask. And please don't ask me to reveal anything that I have had to do to survive - that would be most unfair. I have drawn a line under everything that has happened since you have been away and I expect you to do the same. So when you step through those gates you must leave the past three years behind you, as I will too, and we can take up our lives together as though you had never been away.

I know you may find it difficult to re-adjust to living a normal life again and I am sure that it will take us both some time to feel comfortable in each other's company after so much time apart. I will do my best to make you feel at home. I have prepared the house, taken down the photographs of the children and hidden them in a drawer so that you won't have to feel the pain of seeing them there and knowing that they are dead. I kept them in the drawer for two years after they had been killed and it was only then that I could bring myself to look at them again. I know that when you went away, the house was filled with childish chatter and laughter. It is quiet now and that may be strange for you. I remember that the house seemed cold and empty to me after you had gone and the children were no more.

The worst thing, I knew, would be explaining to you face to face. Perhaps that was why I wanted to run away. I don't think anyone can understand fully how these things happen and I can never tell you the full truth so I will stick to what I wrote to you in the letter. It will be better that way and whatever anyone ever says to you about me, just believe me when I tell you I did what I had to in order to survive. Our life together when you returned was more important than anything else - I knew that you would see that. And we can always make more children together, can't we?

It was unfair of them to make me chose, I know that. I had to decide whether to feed the little ones or myself and I had to keep myself strong for when you returned. Then, when they began to get sickly, there was no medicine after I had spent the money on my new dress. The neighbours said that I should put the children first. The shunned me but I didn't care. I only wanted you to come home - wanted to be strong for you, attractive, as I was when you went away. Having those two around me, demanding and whining was a strain so I ignored them thinking that if I pretended they weren't there that they would go away. Well, they did in the end - they went away for good and I was - sad. Yes, I did miss them and felt regret as soon as I got the first letter from you afterwards. How could I explain to you what had happened? I confess I didn't tell you the complete truth about their deaths. Still you were away and it didn't matter any more. I just wanted you to come home.

And there you are - walking through the gates, looking for me and smiling.

www.ingramcontent.com/pod-product-compliance
Lightning Source LLC
Chambersburg PA
CBHW071538100726
47908CB00004B/1428